SECRET
of the
LOST PLANET

★

ANGUS MACVICAR

BURKE ★ LONDON

To
Helen Kerr

Published by
Burke Publishing Co. Ltd.,
55 Britton Street, London, E.C.1.
Printed in England by
C. Tinling & Co. Ltd.,
Liverpool, London and Prescot

CONTENTS

CHAPTER I

The Broadcast

ONE DAY, about a month after Asa's arrival, a reporter from the BBC called on us at Inverard. We had been testing the new motor. Uncle Lachlan and Spike were annoyed by the interruption. Every minute was precious, for our plan was to take Asa back to her father on Hesikos before Christmas, and we had lost the services of Professor Bergman, recovering from an illness in Sweden. Janet and Madge and I, however, were impressed by our visitor, an eager but well-mannered young man called Max Davidson. Unlike the newspapermen who had badgered the life out of us during the past few weeks, he treated us as sensitive human beings and not merely as pegs for sensational "copy". Asa liked him, too, and readily agreed to his suggestion that as the first living person from outer space to visit the Earth she should give a broadcast interview.

A fortnight later, accompanied by Janet, Asa went to Broadcasting House in Glasgow; and that evening the rest of us gathered in the library to listen. At two minutes to eight I switched on the radio.

'Poor Asa,' murmured Madge. 'I wonder if she's scared?'

Spike grinned. 'Not half as scared as Janet, I reckon. She'll be the coolest of them all there in the studio.'

'I'm inclined to agree with you.' Uncle Lachlan rubbed his craggy chin. 'She's the most self-possessed young lady I've ever met. Her training on Hesikos accounts for it, I suppose.'

The interval bells faded out, and the voice of the announcer came on the air: 'This is the BBC Home Service. In Scotland this afternoon we welcome the girl from the Lost Planet. Here is our special reporter to introduce her to you.'

Max Davidson spoke quietly but with suppressed excitement. 'Some days ago, at Inverard in North Argyll, I sat in Dr. McKinnon's beautifully appointed testing-shed and listened to Miss Asa giving her impressions of the Earth. The group consisted of Dr. McKinnon, who had been busy testing a new atomic motor; his red-haired nephew Jeremy Grant, aged seventeen and already a veteran of space travel; Janet Campbell, Dr. McKinnon's pretty secretary, twenty years of age and a B.Sc. of Glasgow University; Spike Stranahan, his chief engineer, a young American with a broad smile; and Madge Smith, his sharp and sensible Cockney housekeeper.'

'Oh, did you ever 'ear such sauce!' exclaimed our "Cockney housekeeper"; and we couldn't help laughing at her indignant expression.

'And finally,' continued the reporter, 'Asa herself, tall and slim and golden-haired. Asa, daughter of Solveg, the ruler of the Lost Planet. Here she is . . .'

A question crossed my mind. Would Solveg and

Professor Hermanoff, using the Electronome in far-away Hesikos, be able to hear?

'I am happy to be in Broadcasting House,' she told her listeners, 'even though I am not speaking to you at all, as you might think, but merely giving you my thoughts through a process of telepathy common among my people. I will begin by reminding you that it was Dr. McKinnon and his friends who discovered our underground city in Hesikos. We were the last of an ancient race, and though highly skilled in philosophy and the arts—and in the science of electricity—we had become resigned to ultimate extinction in the icy winters of our planet. But Dr. McKinnon convinced us that by using atomic power—which our ancestors outlawed more than a hundred thousand years ago—and by altering our philosophy to regard it as a friend rather than an enemy, we could build up a new world: a world with every scientific advantage but governed entirely by peace and goodwill. When I go back to my father in a few weeks' time I shall travel in a new ship built by Dr. McKinnon and Spike, which will also carry tools and machinery for my people. Meanwhile, as you know, Professor Hermanoff has stayed on in Hesikos to teach our scientists the lost secrets of atomic energy, so that when the machinery comes they will be able to start building at once.'

'Then you think that Hesikos does owe something to the Earth?' put in Max Davidson.

'I do, indeed. And in return, when Dr. McKinnon and his friends visit our planet for the third time,

A*

they will be trained to use the Electronome, a machine invented by my ancestors to send thoughts and ideas through space. Properly handled, this machine could make war unknown.'

'Tell me, Asa, what are your main impressions of Earth? I mean, in comparison with Hesikos."

'I feel much heavier, for one thing! I can't walk or run nearly as fast, because the gravity here is greater, and you have a denser atmosphere.'

'Anything else?'

'I admire your people. They work hard and have a wonderful faith in the future. You have beautiful music, too—something we don't know about in Hesikos.'

'What about our children?'

'Physically they are stronger than we are. They have to be, I suppose, living in towns hidden in smoke and fog, the houses cold and dirty and dark, and the streets filled with rushing vehicles and poisonous fumes.'

'That's certainly a point of view.' Max Davidson was obviously pleased at the way the interview was going. 'Anything else you find strange?'

'Yes—the news in your newspapers. People in every part of the Earth say they believe in peace and friendship, yet they are jealous of each other and continually quarrelling. Nobody seems to think it is wrong for men to grow rich by making weapons— weapons to kill and maim their fellow-beings. But if animals are killed or maimed there is a great outcry. In Hesikos no one has any money, and no one is poor because our wealth is measured by our knowledge.'

'I understand that for thousands of years war has been unknown on your planet?'

'That is so. In your Bible, which I have been reading, there is a splendid phrase: "They shall beat their swords into ploughshares". That is what we have done, and what I hope our example may cause you to do on Earth.'

'Thank you very much.' Max Davidson was almost purring with satisfaction. 'By the way, Asa, have you enjoyed making this broadcast?'

'Yes, indeed. I can feel much love and friendship all around me. But there is something else. I suspect that I have enemies, too—people who are listening now and hating me.'

There in the library we looked at each other in surprise, for Asa's words had become unusually serious. It seemed as if Max Davidson, too, was taken aback.

'Surely not,' he said. 'I really think you must be wrong about that.' Then he brightened. 'And now I will say goodbye,' he went on. 'It was good of you to come to the studio, and we wish you and Miss Campbell a pleasant journey back to Inverard.'

There followed a record of "Over the Sea to Skye", Asa's favourite Scottish tune, and the programme ended.

'My, she was wonderful!' smiled Madge, as I switched off. 'Fancy a slip of a girl like 'er—younger than Janet even—talking like that!'

'What did she mean—that bit about having enemies?' I said.

Uncle Lachlan fished for his cigarettes. 'You know

how sensitive she is to other people's thoughts. She could feel hate, just as we feel the cold.'

'But who could possibly hate her?' demanded Spike. 'Sounds screwy to me, the whole thing!'

'The hate may not be for herself, personally—for her ideas, rather.' Slowly Uncle Lachlan exhaled a spiral of smoke. 'For the past week, in the news-papers, she has been spreading the gospel of peace as she knew it on Hesikos. Now she's done the same on the radio. There may be people on Earth who are afraid of her influence, and who see her as a threat to their business.'

'Surely—surely that's not possible!'

'Preachers of peace and goodwill have been per-secuted before now, Jeremy.'

The telephone rang. Uncle Lachlan got up and lifted the receiver on the desk, while Madge uttered a pious hope that it wasn't someone for supper, because she hadn't even baked a scone.

'Inverard 228 . . . Yes, Dr. McKinnon speaking . . . What! The strange car was actually seen? . . . Yes. Yes, indeed—we'll give the police all the help we can . . . Thank you. Goodbye.'

His face had grown white, and the hand which replaced the phone shook a little.

'What's happened?' I asked.

'That was the BBC,' he said in a grim voice. 'As they left Broadcasting House two minutes ago, Asa and Janet were kidnapped!'

CHAPTER II

Otto Schenk

UNCLE LACHLAN and I went to Glasgow at once, leaving Madge and Spike in charge of the sixty workmen who were fitting the motor in the new ship. We travelled in the jeep, arriving at Broadcasting House just before midnight.

All the BBC could tell us was that the commissionaire had seen two strangers bustling Asa and Janet into a black saloon car which had been standing near the main entrance. He had immediately told the police, giving the registration number of the vehicle, but this was found to be false, and the kidnappers had got clear away. The only bright spot in the picture was that the police had put a close watch on all seaports and aerodromes, and it seemed likely, therefore, that Asa and Janet were still in the country.

We took rooms in a quiet and comfortable hotel in Asia Street; but both of us spent a sleepless night. Next morning we remained indoors, calling the police at intervals and waiting nervously for news. It was all we could do. But we kept on wondering—*why*? Why had Asa and Janet been kidnapped?

Uncle Lachlan became more and more irritable, and I had to be careful what I said to him.

After lunch we were alone in the smoke-room, drinking coffee, when a tall, clean-shaven man came in and sat down opposite us. He was burly, with slant eyes and a yellowish skin, and his thick black hair was closely cut. Once or twice he glanced at us in a speculative way, and I wasn't altogether very surprised when he spoke.

'Good afternoon, Dr. McKinnon. I had hoped to find you here.'

Uncle Lachlan glowered at him. 'Good afternoon, sir. I'm afraid you have me at a disadvantage.'

'And this is your nephew Jeremy? He seems young to be so experienced a traveller in space.'

I acknowledged the greeting.

'A well-mannered boy,' he commented, affably. 'I find that modern adolescents are sometimes apt to be rude and overbearing with their elders.'

'You'll pardon me labouring the point,' said my uncle, 'but have we met before?'

'No, Dr. McKinnon. Even my name would convey nothing to you. It is Schenk. Otto Schenk.'

'H'm. May I offer you some coffee?'

'Thank you, no. But I will smoke a cigar, if that is permitted.'

'Of course. Excuse me mentioning it, but you speak very good English.'

Schenk took a cigar-case from his pocket, and as he did so a small piece of paper fluttered to the floor. He struck a match and began to smoke. 'I am an internationalist,' he explained, 'an agent for several large financial interests.'

'Indeed?' Uncle Lachlan was unimpressed. 'Could you be more specific?'

'Why not?' The stranger smiled. 'My employers are armament firms. On the continent.'

'And you wish to see me in connection with—your agency?'

'In a way. I have come because I may be able to help you to find the missing girls.'

In the street outside traffic murmured past the windows. But in the smoke-room there was a moment of utter silence, like a "still" inserted in a moving film.

'You mean Asa and Janet?' I blurted out.

'Yes.' He inclined his head, with apparent courtesy. 'Those are their names, I believe.'

Uncle Lachlan was staring. 'How can you help us?' he exclaimed. 'Do you know where they are?'

'We've been making inquiries everywhere!' I put in, excitedly. 'And so have the police.'

Schenk made a deprecatory gesture. 'I was under the impression that the Scots are a cool and sober race. It seems I may be forced to revise my opinion.'

'Cut the cackle, will you!' A pulse beat in the angle of Uncle Lachlan's jaw. 'If you know where they are——'

'One moment, Dr. McKinnon! I *may* know where they are. Or I may not. It depends on you.'

'On me? How?'

'Let me explain.' He drew on his cigar. 'My employers would like to gain possession of this remarkable machine invented by the people of Hesikos—the Electronome, as you call it. The proposition I have in mind is that you should leave at once for the Lost Planet, in the space ship you have just built, bring back the Electronome and hand it over to me. When that is done I shall tell you where Asa and Janet may be found. To ensure the safety of his beloved daughter I am sure that Solveg will be glad to let us have the machine and all the secrets of its construction.'

'I see.' Uncle Lachlan spoke slowly, anger draining the colour from his face. 'I—I cannot find words to describe you, Herr Schenk!'

'Please, please! You are being crude—and un-reasonable.' Mockery and cunning were blended in the smooth voice. 'My employers, I may say, are in the process of building a space ship, too—some-where in Europe. They are fully prepared to send armed men to Hesikos, to take the Electronome by force. But this method is so much simpler—so much more civilized.'

'What if we refuse to accept this—this simple and civilized plan?'

'That would be most unfortunate for Asa and Janet. And in the end we should get the Electronome in any case—by sending a ship to Hesikos and taking it by force, as I said.'

'Why are you so eager to control it?'

'I will be frank.' Schenk waved the cigar. 'In the hands of a foolish idealist like yourself—sending out weak-kneed messages of peace—it would make weapons useless and obsolete. In our hands, con-stantly spreading warlike ideas in the minds of men, it will ensure our prosperity.'

'You are frank, indeed, Herr Schenk.' Uncle Lachlan, I realised, was finding it difficult to speak. 'Without a doubt you are the most evil man that I have ever known.'

Our visitor shrugged his shoulders. 'Dramatics are unnecessary. But I do recognise that my proposal must come to you as something of a shock. I will give you time to think it over. To-morrow—at mid-day—I will telephone, and you may give me your answer then.' He prepared to leave. 'Meanwhile, I must warn you not to get in touch with the police. For instance, if I discover that I am being followed when I leave this hotel, so much the worse for Asa and Janet.' He paused at the door and smiled in my direction. 'You must persuade your uncle to be reasonable, Jeremy.'

Uncle Lachlan sprang from his chair. 'Get out!' he thundered. 'Get out before I strike you!'

'That would be inadvisable,' said Otto Schenk. '*Most* inadvisable . . . Au revoir, then—till to-morrow at mid-day.'

The door closed. It was a bitter moment, for apparently we could do nothing without endangering Asa and Janet, wherever they might be. We were helpless, and Schenk knew it.

But suddenly a thought occurred to me and I went down on my knees. 'Did you notice, when he pulled out his cigar-case, something fell under this chair?'

'I didn't. What was it?'

'A slip of paper. Yes, here it is.'

I got up, dusting the knees of my flannels. My find

proved to be a receipt for petrol, issued by a garage in Langbank.

'Langbank? Let's see.' Uncle Lachlan held the paper in one hand and nursed his chin with the other. 'Isaac McNiven & Son, Garage Proprietors, Langbank, near Greenock. To five gallons petrol—one pound, two shillings and sixpence. And the date is today's . . . Jeremy,' he rapped out, 'Schenk came here in a car, so he must have filled up at Langbank only a few hours ago.'

'You think Asa and Janet may be hidden in Langbank?'

'I don't know, but we can find out. Come on—it's only half an hour's run from here. We'll take the jeep and have a word with Isaac McNiven.'

'Oughtn't we to tell the police?'

'Not yet. Schenk warned us about that. In any case, if we're going to take him by surprise we'll do better on our own.'

We drove fast along the docks, past Renfrew Airport and out into the country. On our right was the Clyde, steel-grey under a scud of rain. On our left were damp stubble-fields lately emptied of their harvest.

Dumbarton Rock loomed up on the opposite side of the river, and we went steeply downhill into the village of Langbank. Not far from the railway station we spotted a sign: ISAAC MCNIVEN & SON.

Though in a modest way of business, the firm was obviously efficient, for the pumps were smartly painted, and when we pulled in beside them an attendant in a white coat appeared at once. He

was quite young—only a few years older than myself.
I imagined, therefore, that he might be Isaac Junior.

He took our order and set the pumps in motion.
'Better day now,' he remarked, conversationally.

My uncle nodded. 'Mercifully the rain's gone off.'

'Going through Greenock?'

'No. As a matter of fact we're looking for a friend
who lives hereabouts. I wonder if you know him—
tall, clean-shaven, sallow-skinned, with rather slant
eyes?'

'Slant eyes?' The attendant stopped the pump and
replaced the cap on our petrol-tank. 'Speaks with a
slight foreign accent, does he?'

'That's the man.'

'He was in for petrol this morning. Stays at the old
castle up on the hill—or so the postman says . . .
That's your three gallons, sir. Any oil?'

'No thanks. How much?'

'Thirteen and six.'

'Sorry—I've got nothing less than a pound note.'

'That's okay. I'll get the change at the office.' He
moved off.

'Did you hear that?' said Uncle Lachlan, quietly.
'Schenk is *staying* here!'

I felt excitement creep along my back. 'Yes. And
an old castle's just the kind of place he'd use to hide
Asa and Janet.'

The attendant reappeared. 'Six and sixpence
change, sir. And your receipt. Thanks a lot.'

'Tell me—how exactly do we reach this old
castle you were talking about?'

'Turn left past the station. It's about three miles

off the main road, among a lot of trees. Been empty for years—till three weeks ago, when this friend of yours took over. Kind of a scientist he is, according to the postman.'

'H'm—yes. A kind of scientist. That describes him pretty well.'

'Bit of a hermit, too, it seems. All his own servants from down south.'

'I'm afraid he *is* rather eccentric. We're only business friends, you know. Anyway, thanks for the information.'

'That's all right, sir. Goodbye.'

CHAPTER III

" *Over the Sea to Skye* "

WE FOUND the side-road easily enough and took the jeep part of the way uphill. Then we left it hidden in a disused quarry and continued on foot. The road was lined with hawthorn hedges, behind which we could take cover if any vehicle came along. But nothing passed, and it was almost dusk when we reached the main gate of the castle.

The gate itself was locked—and padlocked with a rusty chain—but we climbed over the high wall and made our way through the wood. It was growing darker every minute, and I was afraid we might get lost. Some instinct guided us, however, because after about a quarter of an hour we reached a clearing and saw the castle in front—a huge dark shadow in the moonlight.

For a time we stood motionless under the trees, waiting for any sign of life. But there wasn't a sound, except for the owls. Not even a light in the castle.

Finally I suggested that if we moved round to the opposite side of the building we might find something, and Uncle Lachlan agreed. As silently as we could, therefore, we picked our way through the tree-trunks. Once or twice we stepped on twigs concealed in the thick grass, but the sound was muffled and carried no threat of danger.

As we had hoped, lights did appear on the other side—one on the ground floor and one two stories up.

Uncle Lachlan put his hand on my shoulder. 'I think we should make a reconnaissance. There's a lawn running right up to the ground-floor window, so nobody ought to *hear* us. Someone may spot us in the moonlight, but we'll have to risk that.'

We crouched down and ran across the lawn, avoiding the beam of light. Then we straightened up and from the side cautiously approached the window. At last I risked looking inside.

It was a big room, like a study. Sitting at the desk, writing, was Otto Schenk.

'Couldn't we break in and overpower him?' I whispered.

'No,' said Uncle Lachlan. 'Before we reached him he'd probably have rung that bell and called in half a dozen of his men to overpower *us*. In any case, we don't know for certain that Asa and Janet are here at all.'

That was sensible—and true. But it was a rambling old place, almost certainly honeycombed with dark corridors, and if once we got inside I imagined we might not be at so serious a disadvantage as he thought.

Suddenly there was music. It gave me a start, floating out of the dim silence, and at first I wasn't sure where it was coming from. Then I realised it was a piano being played in the lighted room on the second floor.

'D'you recognise the tune, Jeremy?'

'Yes. It's "Over the Sea to Skye", Asa's tune. They may be prisoners up there!'

The playing stopped. Peering in at the edge of the ground-floor window, I saw that Otto Schenk was still working at his desk. My hand touched cold metal behind me, and an idea suggested itself.

'Uncle Lachlan, I could climb up this waterpipe. It runs past the window of that room.'

'Looks dangerous, doesn't it?'

'Might be dangerous for you, but I'm a bit lighter. You could stay here and keep an eye on Otto Schenk—and whistle to me if he leaves the room.'

I could see him smiling. 'Quite a planner, aren't you? Very well, Jeremy—but make as little noise as you can. The walls are thick, and it's unlikely that Schenk will hear you climbing, but you never know.'

The waterpipe was clamped about two inches out from the wall, so I could grip it easily. There were plenty of footholds, too, in the interstices between the large stone blocks of which the castle was built, and it wasn't long before I was up and level with the window. I looked in over the sill. At first the light dazzled my eyes, but finally, with a sigh of relief and excitement, I saw them. They were quite alone. Janet was sitting on the piano-stool, crying, and Asa was trying to comfort her.

I tested the window, but it was fastened, and I knocked gently on the pane. The girls started up in surprise, and Janet came running to raise the lower sash.

'Jeremy!' she breathed. 'I—I can't believe it! Oh, Asa, it's Jeremy!'

'I told you he was near us. I could feel it.'

'You're all right?' I asked. 'Not hurt or anything?'

Janet brushed away tears with a small handkerchief. 'No, we're perfectly all right, but——'

'Come on, then,' I interrupted, afraid she might start crying again. 'You're supposed to climb down this waterpipe. Uncle Lachlan's waiting at the bottom.'

Janet came first. Balancing myself against the window, I helped her to slide over the sill and catch the pipe below. Then I did the same for Asa, who remained remarkably cool and said it reminded her of when she climbed down the airshaft to rescue Spike and me from the underground river. I was afraid she might forget that her weight was more than in Hesikos and take too casual a grip of the pipe, but she seemed quite strong and confident.

Suddenly, when the girls were about half-way down and I had just begun to follow, a quiet whistle came from below. My heart missed a beat, and in a whisper I urged Asa and Janet to hurry. As soon as I heard them reach the lawn I jumped down after them.

Uncle Lachlan steadied me. 'Schenk left the room a few seconds ago. He may go upstairs and find his prisoners gone. Then we'll be in trouble. You girls all right? Good. We must get out of the grounds at once and back to the jeep. Keep well down as we cross the lawn.'

The thud of our footsteps as we ran for the wood

seemed dangerously loud; and as we reached the trees a strident alarm-bell began to ring in the castle, and we realised that Schenk must have discovered the escape.

We huddled in the undergrowth, while the insistent bell jangled every nerve in our bodies. Then abruptly it stopped, and we were beginning to move away again when a sound made us turn. The front door of the castle had opened, sending an arm of light almost to the wood. And in that moment a feeling of horror came to me. Silhouetted against the light were three men. One held in leash an Alsatian dog, and as we watched he let it loose.

'Get behind this bush here—and lie still!' Uncle Lachlan's voice was tense. 'If we ran for it now they'd hear us moving among the trees.'

We did as he ordered, peering through the screen of twigs at the Alsatian, which was casting about on the lawn. Schenk's voice came to us, issuing orders: 'Round the back, Kukelheimer—cut off their retreat to the main gate. Petrov and I will follow the dog.'

It took some time to pick up our scent. We were beginning to think that after all it mightn't find us, when all at once it looked up from the grass and made a quick run in our direction. It barked, and I saw its teeth gleaming in the moonlight.

Janet sobbed and clutched my arm. Asa whispered: 'Don't be afraid, Janet. I think I can make friends and tell him what to do.'

I remembered her skill in taming and understanding the birds and animals in Hesikos; but there was no time to consider the position further, for with an angry growl the dog burst in through the bush and stood snarling above us.

Asa put her hand on its head. 'Quiet, quiet. You wouldn't hurt us, would you?'

The thing was a miracle. The dog quietened at once and put its muzzle down and licked Asa's face. She murmured: 'You do want to make friends, don't you?' It whimpered reassuringly.

But Schenk and Petrov were almost on us, and there was no time to lose. Asa caught the Alsatian's head between her hands: 'Off you go now,' she commanded. 'Keep on barking at the other side of the castle till we get away.'

It understood. I don't know how. She had a power of conveying her thoughts to animals, just as she and her people could make them known to human beings. The dog gave a little bark of farewell and darted off around the fringe of the wood, leading Schenk and his companion away from us.

There was a trickle of sweat on my forehead, which now grew cold and clammy. I heard Janet and Uncle Lachlan sighing with intense relief.

'I—I wasn't sure if I could speak to an animal on Earth,' Asa confessed.

'You did it, anyway.' Uncle Lachlan scrambled to his feet. 'Come on—let's get away while we can. We'll climb the wall as far as possible from the main gate.'

'I hope the jeep's still where we left it,' I said.

Uncle Lachlan led us through the trees. 'Asa is our mascot. I don't think anything will go wrong now.'

And as it turned out we did get back to the jeep with no more trouble, and I breathed freely again when we left the village of Langbank behind and sped along the road to Glasgow.

Late that night we arrived at Inverard, where Madge and Spike had an eager welcome for the girls. After supper we discussed the situation.

'Wot I say is, thank goodness Asa can talk to animals.' Madge handed round the coffee. 'But providence was with you, too.'

Uncle Lachlan nodded, and Asa said quietly: 'For a moment I was frightened.'

'Poor Asa,' sympathised Madge, putting an extra spoonful of sugar in her cup. 'But all's well that ends well, as my mother used to say every time the old man went back to sea. . . Did you tell the police, Dr. McKinnon?'

'We did—just as soon as we got clear away from Langbank. They raided the castle an hour later, but by that time Otto Schenk and his friends had all disappeared. They had a helicopter, the police think, which would take them back to Europe.'

'That's right.' Janet was more cheerful and confident now. 'When the two men were taking us in the car from Broadcasting House to Langbank, we heard them mention a helicopter. They'd hidden it in the wood.'

Madge sniffed. 'They're fit for anything, that crowd!'

After a time Spike put into words what all of us were thinking. 'Now that Asa's safe, d'you reckon Otto Schenk will decide to go ahead with his alternative plan and try to take the Electronome by force?'

'I'm pretty sure he will,' said Uncle Lachlan.

Asa looked anxious and hurt. 'It's so hard to believe! No one in Hesikos would be so wicked.'

'I know.' My uncle's face took on a craggy determination. 'And we can't allow him to get away with it. We must warn your father in good time.'

'You mean we'll take off for Hesikos sooner than you intended?'

'Yes. As far as Jeremy and I could gather, the enemy ship isn't quite ready. But to make certain of reaching the Lost Planet before Otto Schenk, I must warn you all to be ready to leave in seven days from now.'

CHAPTER IV

The Testing Time

IN THOSE seven days we all worked like beavers to get the ship ready and to load it not only with food and comforts for ourselves but also with the tools, machinery and atomic models which would help the people of Hesikos to build a new life for themselves.

As Professor Bergman was convalescent in Sweden and would be taking no part in this expedition, Uncle Lachlan had to do most of the paper work himself. He was in one of his old "driving" moods and gave nobody any peace.

One afternoon he sent me down to the testing shed to get some figures from Spike. He didn't say they were particularly urgent; and on the way back I felt so tired after having worked all night—and the weather was so sunny and warm—that I sat down by the little burn in the garden and somehow fell asleep. Ten minutes later I woke up and raced for the study.

I knocked and went in, and at once it was apparent that Uncle Lachlan was annoyed. Janet, typing at a table behind him, gave me a warning look.

'Ah, there you are, boy! Where the deuce have you been all this time?'

I handed over the papers and told him I was sorry.

'I said—where have you been?' he rapped out.

'I fell asleep, down by the burn.'

'You fell asleep! Janet,' he demanded, in a pained voice, 'do my ears deceive me?'

She tried to help. 'Poor Jeremy. He got no sleep at all last night, and——'

'That's no excuse! He's my nephew, isn't he? He's got to work like the rest of us.'

'I know, but——'

He thumped the desk. 'I won't have it, I tell you! Lazy thinking and lazy actions—that's why men like Otto Schenk are able to rule the roost! Don't you realise, both of you—if that man succeeds in capturing the Electronome and bringing it back to Earth, civilisation will be set back two thousand years? Our ship has just *got* to be ready on Wednesday! And it won't be ready if people start going to sleep in the afternoons!'

'I'm sorry,' I repeated. 'It won't happen again.'

'It had better not! Now go down to the ship and tell the foreman engineer I want to see him in half an hour.'

'Right.'

'And when you're there check up on the oxygen installation. Spike tells me there was a faulty valve, but Jock Ferguson ought to have seen to it by now.'

Before I left the room he was dictating more figures to Janet.

Squat and round, like an elongated red balloon,

the ship stood on a concrete launching-platform at the head of the glen. It would have to take off in three days' time, according to Uncle Lachlan, but the scaffolding still clung to it like delicate filigree. Workmen swarmed round its bulging lower hull, putting the finishing touches to the power unit casing.

I climbed the exterior ladder. Inside Asa and Madge were stowing food for the journey. It was an awkward operation, for the ship at rest stood vertically, with the result that the kitchen—and the laboratory—were situated above the central cabin, like attics in a house. After counting the tins and weighing the meat and vegetables, Asa and Madge had to climb up on a step-ladder to pack them in the refrigerator.

When in flight, of course, the interior of the ship would present an entirely different appearance. The cabin would be horizontal and we should walk about on the curved deck without difficulty, rotatory jets giving us artificial gravity. The power unit, instead of being under our feet, would operate behind the control panel at the rear of the ship, and the kitchen and laboratory would be on the same level in the bows. At this moment the various instruments—radar-screens, telescanner, air-conditioning plant and the rest—stuck out from the hull at crazy angles; but when we took off they would all look properly in place.

As I entered the cabin by the open hatch, there was the usual oily smell of metal; and the polished central shaft, round which the ship would eventually spin, gleamed brightly in the artificial light. Above the din of hammering outside I heard Madge talking to Asa.

'That's right, ducks—fifty cans of baked beans. And most of them will be eaten by Mr. Stranahan, I expect. 'E loves baked beans, like all Americans.'

High on the step-ladder, Asa arranged the tins in the refrigerator. 'I can scarcely believe it!' she said. 'In a few days now I'll be seeing my father in Hesikos.'

'So you will, dear—if everything goes according to plan. And everything *should* go according to plan, judging from the racket outside!' She caught sight of me as I crossed the floor. 'Why, 'ere's Jeremy. We thought you were busy with Dr. McKinnon.'

'He sent me to find Jock Ferguson,' I said. 'Seen him anywhere?'

She pointed up, above our heads. In the tunnel housing the central shaft I saw Jock perched on a piece of scaffolding.

'My uncle wants to see you in half an hour,' I called to him.

'Oh, he does, does he? And me in the middle o' packin' this confounded parachute!'

'He's not in a very good mood, Jock.'

'Och, I'll see him, son—don't worry.' The foreman grinned, like a small monkey in a tree. 'I ken fine what he's like! I should be feenished wi' this in half an 'oor anyway.'

I helped Janet and Madge to stow the last of the beans. Then Asa came down the step-ladder, and for a minute we stood talking.

'I wish we were ready to go,' I said. 'I always hate this last-minute rush.'

Madge shrugged her shoulders. 'Rushing about is better than twiddling yore thumbs—that's wot I say. If I 'adn't so much to do I'd be thinking about that awful take-off and getting indigestion most like!'

I couldn't help laughing.

People often expressed surprise that an elderly female cook should accompany us on our space voyages; but Madge was no ordinary cook and no ordinary female. Her father had been a sailor, a member of two Antarctic expeditions, and the spark of adventure in his heart had been transferred to his daughter. Despite her professed fears, she would have been sorely hurt had she been left behind. In any case Uncle Lachlan was only too glad to make her a member of the crew, for her superb cooking and confident control of all domestic arrangements gave the rest of us a chance to concentrate entirely on the scientific and navigational work. At the same time her influence on our morale, when the vastness of space began to daunt us, was invaluable.

A stout and elderly woman had accompanied Captain Cook on his voyages of discovery, a woman who possessed far more of the spirit of adventure than many men. It was the same with Madge. She had no interest in the scientific working of a space ship; but though she tried to hide it behind a smoke-screen of tart common sense, she did love excitement.

At a table in the middle of the floor she began to

B

check more of the provisions, and presently I went across to inspect the air-conditioning system, as Uncle Lachlan had told me. Asa came, too.

As I knelt down by the twin cylinders she said: 'What's it for, that instrument?'

'When we're flying through space,' I told her, 'it balances the air inside the ship. If the oxygen gets too low this valve supplies it automatically.'

'I see.'

Madge's voice came from behind us. 'I wish *I* did, Miss Asa! I just don't try to understand anything. Providence 'as seen me through up till now.'

We laughed, and I went on: 'Watch when I touch this lever. If the valve's all right the pointer on the dial should move to thirty-three point five.'

The needle crept up—twenty, twenty-five, thirty. Then it came to rest at thirty-three point five, and the hiss of oxygen stopped.

Asa clapped her hands. 'It's working perfectly!'

'Yes. Quite okay.' I got up, and we returned to the table. 'I'd better report to Uncle Lachlan and let you two get on with the rations.'

Madge waved a wrapped loaf. 'That's right, son. Dr. McKinnon's orders is that we should finish today, because to-morrow they'll be taking the atomic motor from the shed and fitting it in 'ere— and Asa and I might be in the way.'

'Gosh, yes—to-morrow's going to be bad,' I said. 'Spike will be even more bad-tempered than Uncle Lachlan, I expect—at least until the motor's in. . . Well, I'm off. See you both at supper.'

The next day was Tuesday, and unexpectedly Uncle Lachlan gave Janet and me the afternoon off. I went down to the ship to watch the motor being installed; but Spike and Jock Ferguson told me to make myself scarce, as the cabin was already full of workmen. I climbed back down the ladder, therefore, and sat by the burn in the sunshine, listening to the ripple of the water and the birds singing in the wood and the distant sound of hammering. There was an autumn smell in the air—of damp earth and late chrysanthemums—and it all seemed so homely and peaceful that I almost wished to-morrow's roaring, vibrating leap into space could be postponed.

I threw pebbles into the burn and watched the ripples widen. Suddenly, with a start, I heard Uncle Lachlan's voice.

'Well, Jeremy—day-dreaming?'

I told him I had been sent away, out of mischief, and he grinned and sat down beside me. 'Spike's just about finished,' he said, then added: 'I'm sorry about my bad temper yesterday.'

'That's all right. Thanks for giving Janet and me a holiday.'

'We're inside schedule now,' he explained. 'If the installation of the motor is successful we should have a fairly easy time before the take-off tomorrow. But this journey is so important that I find it difficult to keep my patience.'

He took a twig and broke it in his strong fingers. 'Think of it, Jeremy,' he said. 'Ours is the only space ship in the world—except for the one being built

by Otto Schenk. If we reach Hesikos first we can help
Solveg to fight him. But if he forestalls us, Solveg
will be taken by surprise and may be forced to
part with the Electronome. Schenk would bring it
back to Earth and use it as an influence towards
war. He could become another Genghis Khan,
another Attila, spreading darkness and evil. It must
not happen, Jeremy. No matter what it costs, it
must not happen!'

'But surely it won't be *allowed* to happen?'

'Why not?' The craggy frown returned to his face.
'We are given the freedom of our own wills. If we're
slack and inefficient, evil will take its chance. On the
other hand, if we fight it to the best of our ability,
then we have a moral advantage. That's logic as I
learned it at the University, and I hope you agree
with it.'

For a time I didn't answer; but in the end I decided
to tell the truth. 'I just don't know,' I said. 'I'd have
to work it all out for myself.'

He nodded, slowly. 'Good boy! That's honesty at
least, and I like it!'

A few minutes later Spike came to tell us that the
motor was in position. But it still had to be tested in
conjunction with the jets, and Uncle Lachlan decided
that this ought to be done at once. Jock Ferguson was
summoned, therefore, and instructed to get inside
the ship and close the hatches, while we went to the
observation shelter about two hundred yards from
the launching-platform.

Spike glanced out through the ground-level window of toughened fibre-glass. 'If the jets have the

power we've calculated, Doctor, some of your trees
are going to be blasted out of the ground.'

'I know.'

'Even in a test?' I asked.

'Yeah, sure.'

'Then what happens at the take-off?'

'A good part of the wood hereabouts will be
destroyed,' said Uncle Lachlan. 'But that's a small
price to pay for a ship that will take us to Hesikos,
three hundred thousand miles away, in thirty
hours.'

First of all Spike spoke to the house on the intercom, warning Asa, Janet and Madge to remain
indoors until the test was complete. Then he called
Jock in the ship.

'All set?' he asked.

'Give us a minute to check the main hatch, Mr.
Stranahan.'

'Okay.'

Uncle Lachlan and I went to the window, where
we had a good view of the jets. They were designed
to throw off atomically charged droplets of water, but
the radiation would be absorbed by a screen of
specially manufactured metal behind the launching-
platform. This was one of Professor Bergman's
inventions, and ensured that after a test—and after
a take-off—the ground became safe to walk on within
a few minutes.

Jock's voice blurred through the intercom. 'Right,
Mr. Stranahan. We're ready now.'

'Fine. Motor, please!'

As the foreman engineer handled the controls

inside the ship we heard the noise of the motor rise to a scream, like the wail of a thousand banshees. Then Spike asked for quarter speed, and it died down to a continuous whine.

'Sounds good,' said Uncle Lachlan, with satisfaction.

Again Spike talked to Jock. 'That's grand. Now, when I give the order, switch to Numbers One and Two jets only. The ship will rock a bit, but don't worry, there's no danger of taking off.' He chuckled. 'We'd need the motor at full power and all six jets in action before that could happen.'

'I'll take your word for't!' returned Jock, dryly.

'Ready?'

'Aye.'

'Then switch to jets!'

We waited, and after a moment the whine of the motor was drowned in a muffled roar. We saw smoke and flames hurtle down from the jets like huge waterfalls, splashing outwards against the concrete of the platform. The ship trembled on its supports, and I didn't envy Jock inside. The blast swept twigs and leaves against our window, and almost with disbelief I saw a pine-tree sway and topple over like a cricket-stump hit by a ball.

'What on earth will it be like when we do take off—with all the jets?' I asked.

'Pretty devastating,' replied Uncle Lachlan. 'But we shan't see it. We'll be inside, having our usual black-out.' He turned to Spike. 'That should do,' he said. 'Everything seems to be working well.'

'Fine.' Spike picked up the intercom. 'Okay—

switch off,' he ordered. And as the jets became silent he added: 'That's all for today, Jock. Tell the men to be ready for a final check at six o'clock to-morrow morning. As you know, zero hour's at mid-day.'

CHAPTER V

A Stranger

THAT EVENING, just before supper, I was in the garden, having a look at the little white flowers we'd brought from Hesikos and which Madge called Charity. In the space of a few months they had spread right across the lawn, and now their scent was stronger even than the scent of the pines.

Suddenly I saw Jock coming up the avenue, accompanied by a small thin man dressed in shabby clothes.

'Here's somebody I found at the main gate, Jeremy. Says he's got important news for Dr. McKinnon.'

'Very important.' The stranger spoke with a guttural accent, and his eyes were deep-set and bloodshot. 'Perhaps a matter of life and death.'

I glanced at Jock. 'You know how strict Uncle Lachlan is about callers.'

'Aye. But this chap seems to know Otto Schenk.'

'Yes. My name is Kukelheimer. And I would warn your uncle—he is in grave danger.'

I hesitated, but only for a moment. If this man was acquainted with Otto Schenk it was obvious he couldn't be dismissed like any ordinary visitor. I took him indoors, therefore, and led him to the study.

'Well,' said Uncle Lachlan, grimly, 'what do you want?'

Kukelheimer fingered his small, stubby moustache. 'I have come to warn you,' he said, 'about Otto Schenk.'

'Otto Schenk?'

'Yes. He is planning to destroy your ship.'

Uncle Lachlan frowned. 'Why have you come to me with this story, Herr Kukelheimer? How do I know you're not a spy?'

'I will tell you. Otto Schenk was once my friend. It was I who designed the atomic motor for his ship. But he took the design and paid me nothing, and when I protested—look! Look at my hands!'

He held them up to the light, and I shivered. They were brusied and cut and covered with strips of sticking-plaster. 'He put me in a cellar, below his house. But by main force I pulled my hands from the iron shackles and came to Britain.'

I remembered that a week ago Kukelheimer had been a name called out by Otto Schenk as he searched for us in the grounds of the castle at Langbank. The same thought probably occurred to Uncle Lachlan.

'I see,' he answered. 'When did you come to Britain?'

'Only yesterday. To London. I took a night train at once and came to warn you.'

'About what?'

'If I tell you, how much will you pay?'

'H'm—I thought there might be a snag. Is this blackmail?'

'No, no!' The other spread his hands, apparently

B*

sincere. 'But now I am a poor man. I have no home, no money——'

'All right, all right! I will give you enough to allow you to live in Britain for at least a month.'

'You are kind, Dr. McKinnon. Now, here is my news.' He licked his dry lips. 'Otto Schenk has had trouble with his ship. It will not be completed for several days—and he knows you are ready now. Before I escaped I heard him give instructions. Tonight, when everyone here is asleep, two men are to break into the grounds and destroy your ship.'

'Tonight?' I exclaimed.

'Yes. He knows you have planned your departure for tomorrow. You will have to keep a strict watch, Dr. McKinnon. But there ought to be no danger, now that you have been told.'

Uncle Lachlan pulled open a drawer in his desk and took out some notes. 'If this is true, Kukelheimer,' he said, 'you have earned your money.'

'Thank you, thank you!' Our visitor's gratitude was profuse and embarrassing. 'You are so generous——'

'Cut it out! I don't know exactly why you are doing this, but——'

'Can't you see, Dr. McKinnon—I hate him! I hate Otto Schenk! I would do anything to do him an injury. This is revenge for my hands!'

In spite of his obvious distaste, my uncle was impressed. 'Maybe I'm beginning to understand,' he said, quietly.

Kukelheimer's face was pinched and set. 'There is one thing more,' he said. 'I am a scientist. I designed an atomic motor for Otto Schenk, as I told you, and my whole interest lies in the subject of atomic power. Please—if I could examine your motor before I go——'

'But why?' Uncle Lachlan was again suspicious. 'The design of our previous motor was published in Professor Bergman's book. This one is merely a more powerful development.'

'I know, Dr. McKinnon.' His voice sank almost to a whisper. 'But to see the motor itself—to touch it—that is my wish. Like an artist with a picture by a fellow artist. I cannot explain . . .'

Uncle Lachlan hesitated, then suddenly made up his mind. 'Well, it can't do any harm at this stage. Jeremy—explain the situation to Jock Ferguson and ask him to put guards round the electric fence—immediately.'

'Right.'

'Then ask Spike to come. He and I will take Herr Kukelheimer and show him the motor. Afterwards we'll see him off the premises.'

As I left the room I heard the stranger becoming effusive again. 'Thank you, Dr. McKinnon. You have understood what this means to me. To examine a motor—to see the shining metal and the intricate pattern of the wheels. To smell the oil . . . And perhaps I can help you, too, by describing the kind of motor I have built for your enemy. . .'

After all their hard work, Jock and his men must have been annoyed at having to stand guard throughout the night; but they were sensible enough to see that it was necessary and didn't grumble too much.

I went with Uncle Lachlan and Spike to show

Kukelheimer the atomic motor in the ship. He scarcely said a word when he saw it, but just touched and stroked it, murmuring to himself like a man in a dream. Once, peering down behind the control panel, he took a giddy turn. He staggered and fell, and Spike had to help him to his feet. I felt sorry for him—he looked so thin and frail.

He left us at last, a forlorn figure shambling away from the main gate into the dusk. But he soon passed from our thoughts, for we had more to worry about. All night we took turns on guard with the men, but no one tried to get in, and morning came without anything unusual happening. It helped to take our minds off the journey, I think. At least it did mine, for when my spell of duty was done I slept soundly from four a.m. until nine and woke up feeling quite fresh.

Madge had cooked ham and eggs for breakfast, but I wasn't particularly hungry. Neither was Janet, who could never eat before a take-off but became absolutely ravenous as soon as the voyage began! We both sat nibbling pieces of toast, while Asa quietly enjoyed her meal and Madge talked to us.

' 'E came for the money, nothing else. That Kukelheimer, I mean. 'Is story was all my eye and Betty Martin. Otto Schenk—or wotever 'is name is —'e never meant to send men 'ere. That's wot I say.'

'I don't know.' Janet was unconvinced. 'Perhaps they called it off when they found the place so well guarded.'

'Well, no one could 'ave slipped in last night, that's certain. Wot with the electric fence, and them searchlights, and everyone on guard. Come on, Miss Asa—wot's yore opinion?'

'I agree with you, Madge. I think Kukelheimer came with a false story. But you know, I have a feeling we're in danger all the same.'

'In danger?' said Janet.

'Yes, but I can't explain. It's here inside me— the feeling that something is going to happen.'

'Oh, snap out of it, Miss Asa!' Madge smiled and patted her shoulder. 'Talk about a pessimist!'

I asked her exactly what she meant. Did she think anything might go wrong with the ship? But she shook her head: 'Not that, Jeremy. It's like a threat —something I can't understand.'

Just then Uncle Lachlan came in. It appeared that he and Spike had been looking over the ship and had found everything in order.

'There you are, Miss Asa,' Madge put in. 'It was a false alarm, the whole affair.'

'One of the rotatory jets had developed a short circuit,' Uncle Lachlan explained, 'but Spike soon sorted that out. You'll be aboard by eleven-thirty,' he added. 'Is that quite clear?'

Madge sighed. 'Only *too* clear, Dr. McKinnon! I've a hundred and one things to do yet—including washing up the breakfast dishes.'

Janet and Asa promised to help her. As he left the room Uncle Lachlan said he'd be in the study if any of us wanted him. 'Oh, and Jeremy,' he said, 'you might go along and keep Spike company. Now that there's nothing to do he's fretting a bit. He's down in the garden, beside the burn.'

When I finished my toast I went and found Spike. We sat together on a log, watching our reflections in the water.

'It's a curious thing,' he said, at last. 'You say Asa feels a threat hanging over us. Well, maybe so do I.'

'Gosh, what's happened to *you*?'

'I dunno.'

'But what *kind* of threat? The take-off is dangerous, I know, but we've done it often before, and——'

'It's not that. Dr. McKinnon and I went through the whole ship this morning—practically with a small toothcomb—and everything's okay. Everything.'

'D'you think someone might have slipped in past the guards?'

'No—impossible. Oh, I guess I'm just plain jittery. Kind of anxiety complex after all the hard work.'

His uneasiness was infectious. I tried to conjure it away by remembering how different were the circumstances of this voyage compared with our last. 'I mean, this time we *know* there's going to be danger. From Otto Schenk, if he tries to capture the Electronome.'

But he refused to accept this explanation. 'Solveg should have the answer to that one,' he said.

After a time we were joined by Asa and Janet, who had done what they could to help Madge.

'I'm sorry to be leaving,' Asa said, and as she looked round the garden her long fair hair shone brightly in the sun. 'It's all so beautiful. The green trees and the wet grass—and the scent of the little white flowers. What worries me is that if Otto Schenk comes to Hesikos he may infect us with evil.'

Janet shook her head. 'Dr. McKinnon and Solveg will find some plan to defeat him—I'm sure of that.'

But Asa was doubtful. 'My people are not used to violence. And there is this fear inside me that by some means Otto Schenk has defeated us already.'

'What on earth d'you mean?' demanded Spike.

'I'm sorry,' she answered. 'It may be just anxiety —in case anything goes wrong before I see my father again. It may be that I'm just *afraid*—of the journey through space.'

Spike grinned. 'Well, I reckon none of us would prefer it to a bus ride! But it's twenty past eleven now, so we'd better get cracking. When Dr. McKinnon says we've to be aboard by eleven-thirty, I guess he *means* eleven-thirty!'

We hurried back to the house to collect the things we were taking with us.

CHAPTER VI

Peril in Space

MADGE WAS the last to come aboard, wearing a fashionable tammy and carrying a cookery book for the people of Hesikos. I think she felt their education was neglected because they'd never heard of Yorkshire pudding!

At eleven-fifty we went to our places and fastened our safety-belts. Spike knelt by the controls. These were in the floor as the ship stood pointing upwards; but later on, when we got clear of the Earth's atmosphere and the ship turned and began to rotate, the floor would become the rear wall of the main cabin.

Uncle Lachlan touched a switch and the main hatch rolled over, shutting out the scent of the pines and the glint of warm sunshine and leaving us in artificial light with an oily, metallic smell around us.

'Safety-belts secure?' he asked.

We confirmed it.

'All set, Spike?'

'All set, Dr. McKinnon.'

'Right. I'll have a word with Jock Ferguson.' He lifted the intercom. 'All your men safely in the shelter?' he asked.

'Aye, we're all underground, sir.'

'Nothing inflammable lying about near the launching-platform?'

'I went round myself. Everything's okay.'

'Good. The jets will cause some damage to the trees I'm afraid, but you'll clear up after we've gone?'

'I'll see to that.'

'Keep a listening watch on the light-wave radio, and we'll get in touch with you during the journey and after we land on Hesikos. If you hear that Otto Schenk has taken off, transmit the news to us at once. Each night at twenty-three hundred hours, one hundred hours and three hundred hours. Understand?'

'Yes, sir.'

'If—if anything should happen to us, there are ample funds. You will all be looked after until you find alternative employment.'

'Ach, dinna worry about that. Ye'll be all right.'

'I hope so, Jock. In any case, we're ready now, and the hatch is closed. You may disconnect.'

'Right. Goodbye, sir—and the best o' luck!'

It was two minutes to twelve. As she looked at the clock Asa caught Janet's hand and held it tightly. For some reason she seemed to be even more afraid than prior to her first space journey.

'You all know what to expect.' Uncle Lachlan braced himself against the steel brackets in the wall beside the telescanner. 'At first we shall climb comparatively slowly, but when we reach the stratosphere our speed will have risen to over fifteen miles per second. We shall all have the usual black-out, but it will do us no harm, and when we regain consciousness we shall have escaped from the full force of the Earth's gravity. At first the noise will be alarming, but in outer space there will be complete silence—except, of course, for the hum of the motor running at a tenth of its usual speed. We shall be travelling so fast that the sound of the jets will be left behind.'

The seconds hand of the clock jerked round. Thirty seconds to go.

'Stand by, Spike!'

'Okay, Dr. McKinnon.'

'We have exactly—ten seconds from now. Nine ... eight ... seven ... six ... five ... four ... three ... two ... motor, please!'

Spike pressed a button in the control panel. The motor whined into action, shrieking in our ears. I gripped the buckle of my safety-belt. Asa, Janet and Madge stood together, pale and uneasy.

'Switch to jets!'

Spike's hand went down and pushed over the red lever. For a second nothing happened. Then below us the six jets roared into indescribable fury. The ship vibrated, shocked by their terrific power. It began to lift and sway. Lights flickered and seemed to die, and Asa's face was whiter than her silk blouse. The floor pressed up under our feet like a giant elevator, and I had the feeling of panic which always comes to me at the beginning of a take-off.

The whole cabin heeled over. I had a momentary glimpse of a chaotic, topsy-turvy landscape receding on the telescanner. Then the roar of the jets overpowered everything, and a huge black blanket came floating down . . .

The next thing I knew, someone was shaking my shoulder as I lay doubled up in my safety-belt. Instinctively I noted that the ship had assumed its normal flight position, spinning round the central shaft. I was sitting on what had been the wall before the take-off and what was now the curved floor, on which we could walk without difficulty.

'Come on, Jeremy—wake up!'

I made an effort to obey Janet's instructions, as she helped to unfasten my safety-belt. 'Are we all right?' I said.

'Yes, everything's fine. Asa seems to have been worried about nothing at all.'

'What's the time?'

'Just a minute past twelve.' She smiled. 'D'you know, you're "Tail-end Charlie" again! This time Asa came round before you did.'

I stood up. 'Oh, well,' I mumbled, 'as long as everybody's happy!' Looking round the cabin, I could only see Spike, who was at the controls. 'Where are the others?' I asked.

'Dr. McKinnon's gone to the lab. to make some calculations. Asa and Madge are in the kitchen.'

We went across to the telescanner. The screen was filled by the Earth, riding away from us in dark blue space like a huge patterned ball. We saw Europe and the Mediterranean and across the Atlantic a part of

America curving away; Britain, too, with the west coast hidden under a flimsy wisp of cloud. As we watched, the patterns faded and continents and seas became indistinguishable. We had begun our journey to Hesikos—three hundred thousand miles at ten thousand miles per hour.

Presently Janet and I went to the radar. Our job was to make the flight graph, constructed from regular readings of the flashes on the screens. At the moment, as we sat down, the left-hand screen was showing a flash roughly every two seconds.

'Better start right away,' suggested Janet.

'Right, I'll draw the graph,' I said.

'Okay, Big Chief. First reading. Time—twelve-five. That's your number across. Now your number down. Two point one-five seconds.'

We were more than two thousand miles from the Earth already, and as we continued to mark the readings it became obvious that this was the fastest ship yet. At twelve-twenty the interval was three point five-six seconds, and the graph was developing in a smooth curve.

The hum of the motor was the only sound in the cabin. Spike stood by the controls, watching and noting down the reactions of the various instruments.

After a time Asa emerged from the kitchen with cups of tea. She went into the lab. first, to Uncle Lachlan. Then she helped Spike and finally came to us.

'You angel!' Janet greeted her. 'I've been longing for this!'

'Madge and I were a bit slow,' she confessed,

putting the tray down beside us. 'We were so interested in the new cooker. Hungry, Jeremy?'

'A bit hungrier than I was at breakfast!'

She gave us some chocolate biscuits, which would keep us going until lunch at two o'clock. As we munched them and sipped our tea she sat down to watch the radar.

'This is a wonderful machine, Janet. How does it work?'

'Well, the left-hand screen is beamed back to Earth. As we get farther away the flashes will become fainter, with more time in between. For example, at fifty thousand miles—in five hours from now— they'll occur only once every fifty seconds. At a hundred thousand miles they'll disappear altogether.'

'I see. It's almost as clever as our Electronome!'

'Come off it, Asa!' I said, remembering the pulsing wires and the daunting power which came from it.

She went on: 'And the right-hand screen is beamed towards Hesikos?'

Janet nodded. 'It should remain blank until we get to within a hundred thousand miles of your planet. Then we'll begin to see a tiny flash every hundred seconds or so.'

'That means that for about twenty hours in between we see nothing,' I said, 'unless maybe the Moon or one of the small asteroids. They'll show Uncle Lachlan whether we're maintaining our flight or not.'

She seemed to understand at once; but as she prepared to ask another question we were startled by a shout from Spike.

'Jeremy! Go get your uncle—quick!'

He was standing with his back to the dials and gauges. Under the cold hard light his expression was one of urgent alarm. I put down my tea, therefore, and dashed for the lab.

When I called to Uncle Lachlan from the door he glared up from a note-book in which he had been writing. 'What's the matter, boy? I'm busy——'

'Spike wants you—at the controls.'

'I see.' His manner changed, and he got up at once.

As we ran down the length of the cabin the motor still whispered urgently, without interruption, and I wondered what could be wrong.

We joined Spike. 'Listen!' he exclaimed. 'Close to the panel here.'

Uncle Lachlan and I put our heads against the thin metal. 'There's a ticking sound,' I said. 'Like a clock.'

'Yeah. Behind the starter batteries, I think.' Spike's voice was tense. 'What d'you make of it, Dr. McKinnon?'

My uncle listened for a second or two longer. Then he straightened up, and I saw that his eyes were hard. 'We can't tell for certain, of course. But do you remember, when Kukelheimer stumbled and fell, his right arm disappeared inside the panel here? It was open all the time.'

'I thought of that at once,' said Spike.

'If I'm not mistaken,' Uncle Lachlan went on, quietly, 'Kukelheimer was a saboteur sent by Otto Schenk. He planted a time-bomb—a time-bomb whose mechanism began to work as soon as the motor started.'

CHAPTER VII

Time-Bomb

THE TICKING continued, persistent above the hum of the motor. My imagination began to run riot. Desperately I thought: *at any moment the detonator will go off and the ship will be blown to pieces. . .*

Uncle Lachlan shouted to Asa and Janet by the radar-screens, telling them to stay where they were. Fortunately Madge was in the kitchen, quite oblivious to what was going on.

We began to strip the panelling. It was held together by a series of spring-clips and proved easy to dismantle.

'I never suspected Kukelheimer,' confessed Spike, breathlessly. 'Such a plausible story he told.'

'It was in here he put his arm when he pretended to stumble,' I said. 'We removed these two panels for his special benefit.'

The opening was now wide enough to let us see into the dark recesses of the power-unit, and to avoid any risk of radiation Uncle Lachlan decided that the motor should be stopped.

'But—but then our propelling jet will stop, too,' stammered Spike.

'That is unimportant. Our relative speed will be checked, but we are in free fall and will maintain

our course. Once the jet starts up again we have only
to adjust our navigational figures.'

Spike switched off, and an unnatural stillness fell
upon the cabin. Out of the dark opening the sinister
ticking echoed more loudly than ever. Uncle Lachlan
took an inspection-lamp and shone its beam on the
starter batteries. Suddenly he put his head inside to
look closer.

'See anything?' I asked.

'Wait a minute . . . Yes, there *is* something. A
dark green canister—wedged behind the batteries.
I can't reach it from here.'

'The ship was upright when Kukelheimer came.'
Spike wiped a spot of perspiration from his forehead.
'He dropped it *down*.'

'That's the trouble.' Uncle Lachlan turned.
'Somebody will have to crawl in there and remove
it.'

'But how?' I mumbled, like a fool. 'I mean, it's
stuck tight, and if anyone tries to knock it out——'

'I know. There will be a danger of setting off the
detonator. But it's a danger that's got to be faced.'
He took off his brown tweed jacket. 'We'll have to
strip more of the panelling before I can get in,
Spike.'

I pulled myself together. 'I'm a good deal smaller,'
I said quickly. 'I could get in there now.'

They tried to stop me, but I think they realised at
once that it would save time and that in any case it
was no more dangerous inside the power unit than
in the cabin. If the bomb went off the whole ship
would be destroyed.

I took a hammer and squeezed in, dropping down on the floor behind the panel. Uncle Lachlan shone the inspection-lamp, and I crawled slowly through a maze of wires and machinery. The starter batteries loomed up on my left. Beyond them I saw a round, green-painted object jammed between the side of one battery and the hull of the ship.

'How's it going?' came Spike's voice, echoing in the confined space.

'All right,' I called back.

But it wasn't all right. I stretched out flat and tried to pull the canister clear. It remained fast, however, and the ticking of its internal mechanism, so near and so loud, jarred every nerve in my body.

It would have to be hammered out—that seemed evident. I eased myself up, therefore, crouching on my knees. Then I wedged my shoulders in the narrow space and tapped gently with the hammer. The bomb didn't move.

I was scared to death. Sweat oozed on my forehead, and I had to blink furiously to keep it out of my eyes. I pictured what would happen if I tapped too hard and the thing exploded. There would be a sudden roar and a searing flash beneath my arched stomach. . .

I took a grip of myself. With a shaking hand I tapped again. But still nothing happened. I found myself muttering: '*Oh please—please make it move. . .*'

'Any luck, Jeremy?' It was Uncle Lachlan, only a few feet away, but his voice seemed to come from a great distance.

I forced myself to speak. 'Not yet,' I answered.
'Can you move the battery, perhaps?'

'If I did it would only jam the bomb still tighter.
But don't worry. I'll have it clear in a second.'

Don't worry! What a thing to say, when I felt like
screaming in utter panic! But I musn't panic. Their
lives depended on me doing my best—Uncle Lachlan
and Spike, Janet, Asa and Madge.

With an effort of will I struck the canister another
blow—a smarter blow. And as I saw it move, ever
so slightly, the reaction brought more sweat trick-
ling down across my face. Cold sweat: as cold as
ice.

'Quick, Jeremy! You must be quick,' called Uncle
Lachlan, urgently.

'It's moving!' I croaked back.

Again I struck, and it slid along and miraculously
was almost clear. With a surge of triumphant relief
I wriggled back and bent down to wrench it away.
Next moment the fear came back and turned my
muscles to water. *The ticking stopped.*

'Uncle Lachlan,' I shouted, 'the ticking's stopped!'

I caught the desperation in his answer. 'Then get it
out—*at all costs!*'

I dropped the hammer. I clutched the bomb in
both hands. Savagely I jerked it free; then, panting,
turned and slithered back towards the opening.
Each moment I expected it to burst in my face.

As I clambered through into the main cabin
Uncle Lachlan took it from me. He examined the
surface. We waited, knowing that in a few seconds
now it was sure to go off.

He unscrewed a metal cap. 'Here's the detonator,' he muttered. 'Spike—give me that spanner!'

I watched him at work. My whole world was concentrated in the small cylinder of metal with the powder-filled hollow inside. I was conscious neither of the lights nor of the deadly silence. Only Uncle Lachlan's hands were real—strong, sinewy hands plying the spanner and loosening the rusty nut.

Then the nut was off, and the detonator-unit and clockwork mechanism were separated from the main charge. I could scarcely believe it.

'That should be safe now,' said Uncle Lachlan, breathing like a man after a race. Then he threw the detonator into an empty corner of the ship. 'Stand back,' he ordered. 'There's bound to be a small explosion——'

The explosion came, but it made little more noise than a Christmas cracker and caused no damage at all. I leaned up against the panelling, struggling with a terrible feeling of tiredness. Spike caught my shoulder and steadied me.

The girls came running. 'Dr. McKinnon—what is it?' cried Janet.

Gently he laid the now harmless canister on the floor. 'Kukelheimer planted a time-bomb behind the batteries, where it was most difficult for us to find it. But Jeremy went in and got it out, and now—now it's been neutralised. That small explosion was merely the detonator going off.' He turned to Spike. 'Come now,' he said, gruffly, 'we're back to normal. Better start the motor again.'

'Yeah, sure. I'll fix the panelling as well.'

Presently the quiet hum of the motor filled the cabin. It was the sweetest music I had heard for a long time.

CHAPTER VIII

The Message

ALL THAT day and for most of the night the ship flew on, safely and smoothly. The line on the graph lifted farther and farther away from the small black circle which represented the Earth. Then it began to move down again towards the spot marked "Hesikos". We listened in on the light-wave radio at eleven p.m. and at one o'clock in the morning, but there was no signal from Jock Ferguson at Inverard.

At three o'clock we planned to listen in again—at least Janet and I did. It was our turn on watch. Spike dozed at the controls, Asa and Madge were asleep in the kitchen, and Uncle Lachlan was resting in the lab. Nothing showed on the radar-screens, for we were in the middle of our journey and more than a hundred thousand miles rom the Lost Planet. We sat beside the radio, therefore, watching the hands of the electric clock move silently round. was quiet and comfortable enough, if one could forget that outside there was nothing but dark and freezing space.

At five minutes to three I switched the set on, though it seemed unlikely that Jock would have news for us so soon. Kukelheimer had said it would be several days before Otto Schenk was ready. On the other hand, could we depend on Kukelheimer's word, after what had happened?

'You know, Janet,' I said, abruptly, 'I can't help thinking it's a pity we ever went to Hesikos at all. I mean the first time.'

She looked surprised. 'What on earth's come over you?'

'The Hesikians were happy and at peace,' I went on. 'Then we published stories and books about them —and about the Electronome. Now Otto Schenk will invade the city with soldiers, shooting and killing, perhaps. It would have been better if we'd left them alone.'

'I don't agree. If we'd never gone to Hesikos, Solveg and his people would be dead by now. If you and Spike hadn't blown up the rock in the underground river their electricity would have been cut off and they'd have perished in the cold. Besides——'

'H'm—well spoken, Janet!'

We turned round, startled, to find Uncle Lachlan standing behind us. Our argument had been so engrossing that we hadn't heard him come from the lab.

'I—I thought you were asleep,' I said.

He sat down. 'I came to find out if there was a message from Ferguson.'

Janet told him there was nothing yet, and added: 'Were you listening to what we were saying?'

'Yes. And I'm sorry to say I think Jeremy was talking nonsense. I entirely agree with you, Janet.'

He was smiling, and I felt a shade annoyed. 'But

if it wasn't for us Otto Schenk would never have known about the Electronome,' I reminded him.

'If it wasn't for us the people of Hesikos would now have perished—as Janet said. Otto Schenk may be planning to attack them, but if they want to live a new and better life they must fight for the privilege. We will help them.'

I was beginning to see what he meant. But before I could again rally to the argument there was a slight stutter on the radio. I was pretty sure it was Morse, and we leaned forward to listen.

After a moment the sound occurred again. 'It's Morse all right!' said Janet, opening her notebook. *Inverard calling ship. Message begins. Report on European radio: space ship took off midnight. Thought to be Otto Schenk with troops. Message ends.*

The crackle faded from the loudspeaker, and after a moment Uncle Lachlan switched off. His face was craggier than ever. 'Troops!' he muttered. 'Then Otto Schenk means business!'

'And according to the time he took off,' I said, 'he'll land on Hesikos only twelve hours after we do.'

'It's possible—though his ship may be slower than ours.'

Janet looked worried. 'How are we going to stop him capturing the Electronome? We have no arms. Neither have Solveg and his people.'

'Arms are never the most powerful weapons,' he answered. 'But I must think, Janet. I must think. . .'

The journey went on, minute succeeding minute and hour succeeding hour. We all managed to snatch a little sleep, but it was restless, anxious sleep, and by the time we came to within five thousand miles of the Lost Planet we were all tired and stale.

The air in the cabin, thanks to the excellent pressure-system, was as fresh as ever; but somehow the hard lights were beginning to sting our eyes, and our tempers were becoming edgy and uncertain.

Over thirty hours after the take-off Janet and I were sitting by the radar, struggling with the graph.

'Right, Jeremy,' she said, 'just two more readings.'

'Okay.'

'Time—six-twelve. Interval—four point nought-six seconds. Got it?'

'Yes.'

'Stand by for another . . . time—six-thirteen. Interval—three point nine-seven seconds.'

'Right. The line's moving directly down on Hesikos.'

'Good!' She sighed and leaned back. 'Oh, well, that's that. Gosh, I'm tired!'

'Never mind, Janet. In another twenty minutes we'll be there.'

She nodded. 'Later than Dr. McKinnon thought at first. Stopping the motor put his calculations out a bit.'

'I only hope we'll have time to plan something with Solveg and Professor Hermanoff before Otto Schenk arrives.'

'I'm pretty sure his ship isn't as fast as ours,' she said. 'And have you thought—we have him at a disadvantage now. He probably thinks we were

blown to atoms soon after we took off. He'll be surprised to find us on Hesikos.'

'There's that, I suppose. He was jolly clever,
though. If the bomb *had* gone off, no one would have
suspected him. We'd simply have disappeared in
space, and people would have thought it was an
accident.'

Asa and Madge came with coffee. 'Just a cup
before landing,' Madge explained. 'My,' she went on,
'I'm looking forward to seeing 'Esikos again! And
my old friend, Professor 'Ermanoff. Miss Asa's all
excited, too, thinking of meeting 'er father!'

'It's wonderful to be coming home,' Asa agreed. 'If
it wasn't for Otto Schenk.'

I told her she shouldn't worry, and Madge put in:
'Leave it to Dr. McKinnon and Mr. Solveg, ducks—
that's wot I say. If ever a man 'ad brains it's Dr.
McKinnon, and yore father 'as 'is own share, I
shouldn't wonder!' She helped us to sugar, then
lifted the tray. 'We'll take a cup to Mr. Stranahan
now. Pore Mr. Stranahan—'e's worn out! Never
once 'as 'e left those little clocks and levers of 'is . . .
Oh, and Janet—Dr. McKinnon says everyone to be
in their safety-belts by 'alf-past six sharp.'

'Right, Madge. We'll be ready.'

Fifteen minutes later we stood in our places, while
the round bulk of Hesikos came swinging up on the
telescanner. Already we could make out the green
stretches of mossy turf criss-crossed by deeply scored
valleys and dried-up river-beds. Bright sunlight
had taken the place of darkness and twinkling stars.

Madge was wearing her tammy, and as she

fastened her belt she asked if it looked all right.

'Perfect,' replied Janet. 'You suit it awfully well.'

'I 'adn't much time,' she confessed, 'on account of washing up after the coffee. But if I'm seeing Mr. Solveg I don't want to look a fright.'

Uncle Lachlan glanced round. 'The time,' he said, 'is now about six thirty-three. In two minutes we shall be entering the atmosphere of Hesikos, and for Asa's benefit I'd better explain what happens then. First of all I shall release a parachute in the nose of the ship by pressing this stud. At the same time Spike will shut off the rotatory jets. As a result, the ship will swing round with its tail towards Hesikos. At this point there may be a few moments of—well, unpleasantness. But when the jets come into action as air-brakes we ought to come down as lightly as a feather, and in proper position for a take-off later on. The hydraulic landing-gear should prevent any serious shock. Quite clear, Asa?'

'Yes.'

'It's all perfectly normal,' he smiled. 'Nothing to worry about.'

Madge asked exactly where we were going to land.

'Close to the mouth of the tunnel which leads to the underground city. Just above the river-bed.'

'So we won't 'ave far to walk?'

'Less than half-a-mile. But I should think Solveg will send someone to pick us up in the jeep we left behind. He's bound to know we're coming.'

Asa glanced at the telescanner, where the pointed hills of Hesikos could now be seen like small ripples on the surface. 'He does,' she said. 'I can feel his thoughts already. He is happy that we are coming back, but he knows there is danger.'

As she spoke there was a slight tremor in the ship, and I saw that the time was exactly six-thirty-five. Uncle Lachlan released the parachute. The cabin swung violently. A pencil I had left near the radar whirled and clattered round the hull.

'Cut rotatory jets!'

Spike touched a lever, and we were shaken as if by a giant hand. The cabin was like the interior of a lift gone mad. The safety-belts kept us from being flung about, but gradually we slid down the walls to stand on a level with the control-panel.

'Switch to main jets!'

'Sure!'

In a moment, travelling backwards into the sound, we heard their comforting roar, and our violent motion was arrested as the jets became air-brakes and supported us like a ball on a sinking fountain. At first there was so much pressure beneath us that we had difficulty in standing upright, but gradually the feeling passed and our descent became smooth and easy.

I watched the dial. Five thousand feet . . . three thousand feet . . . two thousand feet . . .

'Jets off, Spike!'

The switch was thrust over. The whine of the motor and the thunder of the jets faded out to silence, leaving only a faint whistle of wind outside.

Three hundred feet . . . two hundred feet . . . one hundred . . .

I shut my eyes. There was a jarring crash. My

teeth were clamped together; my knees buckled and without the safety-belt I should have fallen. The ship staggered like a drunken man. Then a loud hiss came from the hydraulic landing-gear. We rose up a few inches and became steady and stable.

Gradually I realised that for the third time we had made a successful landing on the Lost Planet.

CHAPTER IX

"*Here is Otto Schenk*"

HAVING UNBUCKLED our safety-belts, we opened the main hatch. Once again, with an odd catch in our throats, we saw the strange landscape of Hesikos—the pointed hills, the pastel-green moss, the little white flowers like snowflakes on a lawn; the blue sky and the rayless sun. There came to us the wonderful scent of the place, lapping round us with such friendliness and peace that it was difficult to believe a man like Otto Schenk existed.

We climbed down the ladder. Because of the decrease in gravity I jumped the last dozen rungs and scarcely felt myself touching the turf. Half a mile away was the hill with the tunnel leading down to the underground city; and coming towards us from the tunnel, moving fast among the pink rocks, we saw the jeep. As it came closer we recognised the driver—tall, fair and smiling.

'My, wot a 'andsome man!' said Madge. ' 'Oo is 'e?'

'It's Petra, my father's chief lieutenant' Asa ran forward as the jeep came to a halt a few yards away. 'Petra!' she called. 'Dear Petra—how wonderful to see you!'

All of us had met him before. All of us, that is,

except Madge who greeted him primly: 'How d'you do, Mr. Petra? Pleased to meet you, I'm sure.'

He shook hands with us and spoke particularly to Spike and myself. 'You know, our little boys have a new game. They pretend to blow up the rock in the underground river and quarrel among themselves about who shall play Jeremy and Spike!'

Uncle Lachlan told him we had brought a ship-load of tools and machinery. He seemed pleased and went on to explain that their scientists had been studying diligently since we left, under the guidance of Professor Hermanoff, and were now ready to apply the new atomic principles.

'But that can wait,' he said. 'You had better come and discuss the immediate situation with Solveg. I have room for three in the jeep.'

Uncle Lachlan arranged that he and Asa and Janet should accompany Petra back to the city. Spike and I were to remain in the ship with Madge and keep watch on the radar. With any luck we might be able to pick up the enemy ship as it approached.

'When will you be back?' I asked.

Uncle Lachlan rubbed his chin. 'It depends. Solveg and Hermanoff and I must think out this problem. But I may return in the morning. . . By the way, Petra, is the portable radio in the jeep still working?'

'Yes. Professor Hermanoff repaired it.'

'Good. I will keep it with me all night. If you do pick up Otto Schenk on the radar, Jeremy, transmit a message to me at once.'

'Right you are, Uncle Lachlan.'

It was nearly the time of sunset, and on Hesikos darkness always came down quickly, like a blanket being thrown over one's head. When they rode off in the jeep, therefore, we lost no time in getting back into the ship; and while Madge prepared a meal Spike and I worked out a system of watches for the radar.

The night was long in passing. It was eerie sitting there, looking at the blank screens for minute after minute and hour after hour. Outside it was silent. No life stirred on the surface of Hesikos—not even a breath of wind—and I wished I had been able to go with Uncle Lachlan and share in the movement and thought of the underground city. The main hatch was only partially closed, to give us fresh air, and through the oblong opening I could see the Earth shining in an indigo sky. Inside the cabin it was silent, too, except for an occasional sigh from Madge, asleep on a mattress by the control panel, and the regular deep breathing of Spike, who was muffled up in blankets on a chair beside me.

My second spell on watch came to an end at four in the morning. I wakened Spike, who shed his coverings, rubbed his eyes and stretched.

'Okay, kid—I'll take over. Any luck?'

'Not a thing. But if the enemy ship is only twelve hours behind us, it ought to be showing up by now.'

'Well, I dunno. It's a small object—comparatively speaking. It might not register until it's fairly close.'

I crossed to the chair he had just vacated and began to snuggle in among the blankets. It wasn't cold, but I was glad of their comfort. Everything was so still and quiet that I felt uneasy.

When I mentioned it to Spike he admitted that his own feelings were similar. 'It must be the thoughts of the Hesikians coming to us,' he said. 'On our first voyage their thoughts were peaceful, so we felt at peace. Now they're troubled—so we're troubled, too.'

'It's queer, this thought-transference.' I should have been sleepy, but instead I was alert and wide awake. 'I mean, long before we landed Asa knew what her father was thinking, and she had already sent him news of Otto Schenk.'

He shrugged his shoulders. 'Maybe it's not so queer after all. It's a natural development. Pretty often you know what your uncle is thinking about, don't you—though he doesn't say a word?'

'Well, yes. I can usually tell what mood he's in, anyway.'

'That's the idea. It's a question of practice and concentration. Once the human race is as old as the Hesikians we may be just as far advanced as they are.'

There was silence for a time. The radar remained blank. I tried to sleep, but there was no sign of sleep coming.

'Have you ever thought, Spike—why are men like Otto Schenk *allowed*?'

He turned and grinned at me. 'I'm not sure if

a plain ordinary engineer is capable of answering that one! But are you sure "allowed" is the right word?' He leaned back with a sudden look of seriousness. 'The way I see it, men like Otto Schenk are *put* into the world to *test* the world. It's difficult to explain what I mean. They're like the measles, if you like. Measles test out the strength of the body, and if you come through you're healthier than ever and don't have measles again. Men like Otto Schenk test your character.'

I confessed I had never thought of it like that before.

'Neither had I, kid! I'm just trying to get it straight in my own mind. I reckon Otto Schenk is a kind of test—for us, and for the Hesikians.'

'That's probably true. I'm sure it's how Uncle Lachlan sees it. But does Solveg?'

'Well, there's the rub, as your Shakespeare said!'

He had scarcely finished speaking when I was more wide awake than ever. Faint but unmistakable on the radar there had appeared a tiny flash. We craned forward. Ten seconds later we saw it again.

'Something quite small,' said Spike, trying to conceal his eagerness. 'Let's take a few readings and see what happens.'

I threw off the blankets and got ready a sheet of lined paper. 'D'you think it's the enemy ship?'

'We'll see,' he answered, cannily. Consulting the stop-watch he went on: 'Time—four-fifteen. Interval —ten point-three seconds.'

C*

'Got it,' I said.

Five more readings made it plain that the graph was working out in a regular pattern. The object —whatever it might be—was ten thousand miles from Hesikos but approaching at a hundred miles per minute. It was almost certainly a space ship, which, at its present rate of progress, would land in an hour and forty minutes.

'Ought to be daylight by then?' I said.

'Yeah. It's getting clear outside already.' Spike rubbed his long nose. 'I'm pretty sure it's Otto Schenk,' he continued, 'though he must have been using booster jets to be so close behind us. We'd better get in touch with Dr. McKinnon.'

I switched on the transmitter and let it warm up.

According to plans, Uncle Lachlan would have the portable set beside him in Solveg's house, tuned in to the proper wavelength. After a moment Spike made a call.

'Ship calling Dr. McKinnon. Ship calling Dr. McKinnon. Over.'

He pressed the receiving switch. There was a slight crackle on the loudspeaker but nothing more.

'Ship calling Dr. McKinnon. Ship calling Dr. McKinnon. Over.'

This time we got an answer. 'McKinnon calling ship. Receiving you loud and clear. Over.'

Spike gave the thumbs-up sign. 'Ship calling Dr. McKinnon. Object located on radar. Ten thousand miles away, travelling six thousand miles

per hour towards Hesikos. Think it my be enemy
ship. Over.'

'McKinnon calling ship. From figures given I
calculate time of landing approximately six o'clock.
Do you agree? Over.'

'Ship calling Dr. McKinnon. Landing time
agreed. What are your plans? Over.'

'McKinnon calling ship. Otto Schenk may try to
contact us by radio after landing. I'll be with you
shortly. Over and out.'

For the next hour we followed the progress of
the object on the radar. Nearer and nearer it
came, undeviating in its course; and in the end we
had no doubt at all that it was Otto Schenk's
ship.

'Spike,' I said, once, 'what if he made a crash
landing?'

He smiled. 'That would be one solution. But we
can't depend on it!'

At about a quarter to six we heard the jeep
outside, and soon afterwards Uncle Lachlan joined
us in the cabin. Madge woke up and when told of
the position calmly decided to make us a cup of
tea. While she was doing this we watched the flashes
on the radar occurring closer and closer together
until at last they formed a continuous pattern.

'He's landed all right,' said Uncle Lachlan. 'About
a hundred miles away, I should judge.'

Spike nodded. 'Then there's no immediate
danger?'

'I don't think so. The troops probably have jeeps;
but even so, it would take them at least four hours

to reach us across the rough country. I've a feeling, though, that Schenk may try to contact us before he does anything. Cut the radar, Jeremy.'

I switched it off and tuned in the radio. 'But, Uncle Lachlan,' I said, 'Otto Schenk probably thinks we were blown up.'

'I'm not so sure. In any case, he knows the wave-length we use——'

There was a crackle on the loudspeaker. A deep guttural voice came through, and a finger of fear touched my back.

'Here is Otto Schenk. Here is Otto Schenk. You may think I do not know that you are alive and safe. I *do* know, because my radar did not record your destruction as planned. But it makes no difference. In twelve hours from now I expect to receive the Electronome at my ship, together with a skilled operator to explain its workings. If not, I will come with my men and destroy the city and take the Electronome for myself. Au revoir, Dr. McKinnon. Au revoir.'

Uncle Lachlan switched off. 'I'm pretty certain that's a recording. They probably intend to repeat it every few minutes.'

Spike agreed with him. 'So we have no advantage at all?" he said.

'None. Except that I don't think he knows exactly where we are. And the worst of it is—Solveg *wants* to hand over the Electronome, to avoid trouble.'

I tried to face realities. 'Didn't you tell him what that would mean to us on Earth?'

'I told him, Jeremy, but he's thinking of his own people. However,' he added, 'Schenk said twelve hours. We have at least twelve hours in which to make Solveg change his mind and make a plan. . .'

CHAPTER X

The Pulsing Wires

AFTER CLOSING the main hatch and making
everything safe and secure, Madge and Spike
and I left the ship and went back with Uncle Lachlan
in the jeep, taking with us various small items—
rations, notebooks, maps and charts, a compass,
some sticks of gelignite and a number of presents
for the people of Hesikos.

Down the long entrance tunnel we went, our
headlights blazing; then past the great iron door
which could roll shut at the movement of a switch
and in through the wide gate of the fairy town.
The square, flat-topped houses and level streets,
in a mosaic of pink and white, were serenely
beautiful, basking in the scent of the flowers in their
gardens. The people went about their business
without haste or fuss. The air was fresh and cool,
flowing in through the ventilation-shafts, and over
it all shone a silvery light reflected downwards from
the cavern-dome of shining stone.

As we went slowly through the main street the
tall, pale people smiled, giving us their thoughts in
greeting. The children waved and ran alongside
the jeep, while Madge bowed to them like a duchess.

It seemed obvious that they hadn't yet heard of Otto Schenk's twelve-hour ultimatum.

Asa met us in the central square, and from there Spike and Uncle Lachlan drove on to Solveg's house. But Madge, whose first visit to the city this was, said she'd like to see the Electronome, and Asa and I took her across to the small building where it was kept. We had nothing better to do in the meantime, as it was clear that Uncle Lachlan, Solveg and Professor Hermanoff would have much to discuss before deciding on a course of action.

The door slid open on oiled runners. Inside there was nothing to be seen at first: just a tiled floor on which our shoes made a whispering echo and a small tubular railing at the far end. But beyond the railing was a red light high in the wall, and beneath the red light an oblong box of transparent mica filled with hundreds of gleaming, pulsing wires. We stood by the railing and heard the sound of the Electronome—the quiet *tr-r-r-rick*, *tr-r-r-rick* of the scanning beam as it circled the whole universe. This was the machine coveted by Otto Schenk, the machine which would soon bring trouble and danger to Hesikos.

I tried to explain it to Madge. 'The big dynamo in the power-house, which manufactures electricity—that's what you might call the heart of Hesikos. This is the brain of Hesikos, isn't it, Asa?'

'In a way. Though of course the real brain o Hesikos exists in the thoughts of its people. The

Electronome is only a receiver and transmitter of thoughts.'

Madge was quiet and subdued. 'It's beyond me, this is! You'd think the wires were all alive— like veins of glass with blood pumping through them.'

'That is a good comparison. They're like the cells of a living brain.'

'But—'ow does it work exactly?'

Asa pointed to metal terminals at either side. 'When the Electronome is adjusted to the proper wavelength the operator holds these tightly. His thoughts are then transmitted through the wires, and presently, if conditions are favourable, he receives thoughts in return.'

'It's uncanny, that's wot it is.' Madge gripped the top of the railing with tense fingers. 'Could *we* use it?' she asked. 'I mean, Jeremy 'ere, or 'is uncle, or Janet per'aps?'

'They could—once they had been trained. You see, the operator himself has to know how to transmit thoughts.'

Madge wanted to examine it in more detail, but Asa said it would be dangerous to go closer than the railing.

'As Spike and I found to our cost, when we tried to make a plan of it and nearly got killed!' I said.

'It has a certain power,' Asa went on. 'A radiation of energy, if you like, which might affect the mind of an unskilled person.'

I could sense that power even now: a brooding menace which undermined confidence and courage. Madge felt it, too, and asked what it was.

'It's difficult to explain.' Asa's eyes were troubled. 'In simple language the Electronome is worked by electricity, but its main constituent is iridonium— the metal you know about—which is found only in our planet. Charged with electricity, iridonium creates a field of radio-active power which paralyses an ordinary mind not trained to resist it.'

Madge shivered, but her brain was still alert. 'If it's so dangerous,' she said, ' 'ow could Otto Schenk make use of it?'

'He could be taught by one of our people, within a few weeks. His mind is so clear and powerful that it would only need to be developed along the same lines. Dr. McKinnon and Professor Hermanoff could also learn, just as quickly.'

For a time there was silence, except for the continuous *tr-r-r-rick* of the machine. Power throbbed through the wires in time with the sound.

'Listen to it!' exclaimed Madge, at last. 'Going on and on, as if it were alive!'

Asa took her arm. 'I know. It has been working like that for thousands of years, while my people tried to send thoughts to other worlds. And their thoughts did reach the Earth, centuries ago, when there was peace among your nations and Plato called our world Hesikos, the peaceful planet.'

Madge turned away. 'Peace or no peace, I 'ate it! I 'ate your machine, Miss Asa! It makes me afraid!'

I tried to comfort her by saying I felt the same, but she scarcely heard me. As we left the building she whispered to herself: 'I loved 'Esikos up till now. The clear air, and the 'appiness, and the little white flowers. But there is something 'ateful about that machine. . .'

At Solveg's house we had a meal which consisted mainly of the delicious honey-cakes we had tasted before, washed down by cups of a refreshing drink made from the pear-shaped fruit of Hesikos. Afterwards Janet, Madge and Spike went to visit the home of the birds and animals. This was a beautiful underground dell, with running water and leafy green trees, where the birds could fly and shelter from the cold outside, and the little blind brownies, which so much resembled squirrels, could burrow to their hearts' content.

Meanwhile Asa and I sat on in the big cool room, listening to the discussion between Uncle Lachlan and Solveg and Professor Hermanoff. To my dismay Solveg appeared quite set in his decision to bow to the ultimatum and give up the Electronome to Otto Schenk.

Presently Uncle Lachlan began to lose his temper. 'Surely this is no way for a ruler to talk!' he exclaimed. 'A weak capitulation! A spineless compromise!'

Solveg was tall and fair, with a lined face like an old Greek god. Usually it was calm and happy; but now there was anxiety in his deep-set eyes. 'Dr. McKinnon,' he answered, 'I admire your courage. Nevertheless, my mind is made up. There must be no risk to my people of strife and bloodshed. For thousands of years we have lived in peace, and it would be unthinkable for us to engage in war.'

'But if Otto Schenk gets the Electronome, can't you see what it will mean to us on Earth? Hermanoff, you must support me in this!'

The stout Slav nodded with vigour. 'I support you to the utmost, Dr. McKinnon. Solveg, my friend, for many months now I have lived with you and your people. I have come to admire your calm philosophy, your spirit of charity and good will. For my part, I have worked methodically to teach the principles of atomic power to your scientists; and now Dr. McKinnon has brought tools and machinery. You have been given the opportunity to spread and multiply and build new cities without fear of the winter cold. It is to us—to the people of the Earth— that you owe all this.'

'I admit it. And I am grateful.'

'But the basis of all existence,' Professor Hermanoff went on, 'is co-operation. Surely that is true, even between the planets. We have helped you. Now you must help us. If Otto Schenk is allowed to bring the Electronome to Earth, think of what will happen! You employ it to spread peace and love. Otto Schenk will employ it to create enmity and war.'

Solveg bowed his head. 'I understand this argument, but I must consider the well-being of my people. We can build another Electronome——'

'Certainly you can build another Electronome,'

snapped Uncle Lachlan. 'But it would take years to perfect such an instrument, and by then the damage on Earth will have been done. Don't you remember how Jeremy here—my nephew—how he and Spike Stranahan were willing to sacrifice their lives to save your city, when the great rock dammed the underground river? Are your people not prepared to make some sacrifice for us?'

'You disturb my mind, Dr. McKinnon. But all the same——'

'There is still another side to the argument,' interrupted Professor Hermanoff. 'No race of people can ever advance until they prove themselves worthy of advancement by their consideration for others.'

It was as if Solveg had received a physical blow. He winced and looked down at the tiled floor. For a moment he was silent, his hand to his broad forehead.

Then he looked up. 'My friends, your logic is difficult to answer. But even though I and my people should be willing to help, what could we do against Otto Schenk? We are completely at his mercy. You yourselves have no weapons.'

'That is true,' Uncle Lachlan admitted. 'We are at a physical disadvantage. But you and Professor Hermanoff and I—surely together we have enough intelligence to make some plan of defence!'

Solveg didn't answer, and after a moment Hermanoff said: 'One thought has occurred to me. The Electronome is here, at the very centre of the city. And to the city there is only one entrance—

the tunnel with its rolling iron door. Could your people not fill hundreds of bags of earth and pack them behind that door? Unless he has a plentiful supply of explosives Otto Schenk should then find it impossible to break in, and ultimately he will have to raise the siege, either when food for his men runs short or when the cold of winter forces him to return to Earth.'

'Good for you, Hermanoff!' exclaimed Uncle Lachlan. 'That's talking sense!'

'But there are other entrances,' Solveg pointed out, and I saw that he was trembling. 'The air-shafts, and the river which flows underground to generate our electricity——'

'They can be guarded, and blocked if need be!' cut in Uncle Lachlan, impatiently. 'Solveg, you must see our point of view! We should do the work ourselves, if we had more manpower. But in the time Otto Schenk has given us—twelve short hours—we need assistance.'

Again Solveg put a hand to his forehead. 'I am sorely troubled,' he said. 'But I am beginning to see your position.'

'You'll help us then?' Eagerly Uncle Lachlan leant forward.

'I will tell my people to prepare a barricade on the main door.'

'Well done!'

'But I must remind you—it is against all my principles.'

'We appreciate that—and admire you all the more for it. Meanwhile we must send out a patrol to discover the strength of the enemy and, if possible, his intentions. I will ask for volunteers.'

'No need for that,' I said, quickly. 'Spike and I will take the jeep and do it.'

Uncle Lachlan turned and smiled in my direction.

CHAPTER XI

Night Patrol

SPIKE AND I put a few rations into the jeep and made sure that we had proper sketch maps of the area where the enemy ship had landed. Then we borrowed Uncle Lachlan's compass and under the rear seat packed half a dozen sticks of gelignite in case we met any obstacles on the way.

In about an hour we were in the central square, ready to move off. Spike intended to drive, while my job was to navigate from Professor Bergman's maps; and we calculated that if all went well we should be back in about eight hours.

Solveg and Uncle Lachlan wanted us to find out two things in particular: how many men Otto Schenk had brought, and how they were equipped—their weapons, transport, etc. We had arranged the time of our departure so that we should reach a point within a few miles of the enemy ship by the time it got dark. Then we could leave the jeep and do the rest of the patrol on foot.

Spike and I climbed into the front seat.

'Look after yourselves,' said Solveg, gently. He and Uncle Lachlan had come to bid us *au revoir*. 'And take as few risks as possible.'

My uncle's face was set and craggy. 'Don't forget,' he warned us, 'the enemy ship may have searchlights and other devices for spotting you.'

Spike pressed the starter. 'Okay. We'll look after ourselves——'

There was a sudden interruption. 'Wait for me! Wait!'

Turning, we saw Asa, in her short kilted tunic, racing across the square. She came to us, breathless. 'I only heard just now that Jeremy and Spike were ready to leave. I—I'm going with them.'

Solveg gripped her shoulders. 'My child—are you mad?'

'Not in the least, Father. But I cannot allow Jeremy and Spike to face all the dangers by themselves. Besides, I know the country well—much better than they do.'

'But if this—if this Otto Schenk were to capture you again——'

'Then I'd just have to find some means of escape. I'm no longer a child.' She climbed into the back of the jeep, ignoring rather feeble protests from Spike and myself; then sat down and smiled. 'There —that's quite comfortable, even though the ration tins do have sharp edges!'

Solveg caught her arm. 'But Asa——'

'I'm going, Father. Ever since Dr. McKinnon and his friends first came to Hesikos I have wanted to be like them—brave and adventurous, not prim and quiet, like us.'

'Let her go,' said Uncle Lachlan. 'I should be proud of my daughter if I were you. As your people begin to venture out and build a new life for themselves she will be the one to lead them.'

The older man hesitated; but presently his hands dropped to his sides. 'So be it, my friend. It is difficult for us, as we grow older, to hand the reins to our children. But it must always happen. . .'

Spike let in the clutch.

It was a long journey, trundling over the green moss and carefully avoiding the outcrops of pink and white stone. The flowers which Madge called Charity were sprinkled everywhere, like crumbs on a green tablecloth, and their scent was strong and encouraging.

The enemy ship lay a hundred miles due north, according to the radar, and I used the compass to steer a direct route. On Hesikos, of course, the compass didn't point to a magnetic north, as on Earth. Its needle turned in the direction of the underground city—attracted by the powerful radio-active and magnetic field of the Electronome. As long as we remembered this, it proved effective.

When we had been travelling for two hours we came to the summit of the great cliff which stretched for miles to the east and west. We remembered it well from our last visit, for it was this cliff, as we travelled in the opposite direction, which had presented what seemed an insuperable barrier to further exploration. Then we had found a narrow track running diagonally to the top—a track with the rusty remnants of metal rails which had given us our first clue to the ancient civilisation of Hesikos. On this occasion we drove for about a mile along the summit searching for the track; but we found it at last, looking so steep that my heart was in my mouth as Spike drove down. Apart, however, from a few momentary skids on the scattered patches of loose stones, we reached the bottom without mishap.

For the next hour we sped easily across a flat plain, dotted with small trees bearing bunches of pear-shaped fruit. Here and there we encountered narrow, dried-up river-beds, but the jeep rode across them lightly and without difficulty, as on Hesikos it weighed much lighter than on Earth.

Darkness came on us quickly, spreading in over the pointed hills to the south. Just before it reached us, however, we saw a deep valley in front, with sloping stony sides; and when we stopped and climbed out of the jeep in the gathering dusk we noticed something in the bed of the valley which made our hearts jump with excitement.

'A light!' I exclaimed.

'Yeah.' Spike lay on his tummy, peering down. 'It might be coming from the open hatch of the enemy ship.'

I wriggled forward over a pile of loose rock. 'Hope they haven't spotted us,' I said.

'Not in the dusk, Jeremy.' Asa was confident. 'And in any case, for the past hour we've been travelling across the plain out of their sight.'

As Uncle Lachlan had said, we should have to do the remainder of the journey on foot, and I took a bearing with the compass in case the light went out later on. Then we began the long climb down, among outjutting boulders and shifting screes, reckoning that it would take us about half an hour to reach the light and whatever lay behind it.

A thought struck me. 'What about the jeep? Will it be safe behind that knoll?'

'We'll have to take a chance,' replied Spike. 'But we must make sure the enemy don't cut us off. It's our only means of retreat.'

We were wearing rubber shoes, which was fortunate, because otherwise we should have made a considerable noise scrambling among the rocks. It was so dark that we could see only a few feet ahead, and several times one or other of us almost fell as we slipped on hidden obstructions. Stars were shining overhead like lamps on a Christmas-tree, but they gave very little real light in the valley. For the main purpose of our patrol this was probably just as well. We remained invisible to any watchful eyes down below.

The light we had seen continued to shine steadily, though we could see nothing behind it but a great indefinable patch of dark. As we approached, however, this patch took on an outline, until at last we knew for certain that it was a space ship—a long, slender ship standing vertically on its tail, dark in colour and having more of a conventional design than our own.

Then we heard a humming noise, which almost certainly originated inside the ship. Spike whispered that it might be the atomic motor running at low speed to charge the batteries. We found, in any case, that our first guess had been correct: the light was coming from an open hatch about twenty feet above the ground.

Thirty yards away from the towering bulk of the enemy ship we stopped.

'I can feel their thoughts already,' Asa said. 'Hard, calculating thoughts. But they don't know we're so near them.'

Spike decided that if we moved to the left a little we should be able to see directly inside; and he was right. When we edged round and stood immediately in front of the open hatch we saw what looked like a picture in 3-D. The cabin was brilliantly illuminated. At a table in the centre of the floor fifteen men were seated enjoying a meal. All were dressed in the same kind of uniform: dark shirts and long blue trousers, with high leather boots. Then I spotted Otto Schenk sitting in a corner, making notes beside a radio-set.

Presently we saw two other men. One was stout and burly and wore a striped apron. He was handing round dishes of food and was probably the cook. The second was tall and thin, with gold braid on his jacket: an officer I guessed, waiting for the ordinary soldiers to finish their meal, when he and Otto Schenk could eat together.

'Otto Schenk, an officer, fifteen men and a cook. That's the enemy number—eighteen in all. But what about weapons?' said Asa. 'Can you see any?'

'They have rifles at least,' answered Spike, 'stacked against the rear wall of the cabin. See?'

Asa shivered, her body trembling against my arm. 'That means if they do get into the city we'll have little chance against them?'

'I guess that just about sums it up. But they haven't got into the city yet. The barrier your father's putting up behind the door may be enough to stop them.'

We went closer. There was no sign of a jeep, or jeeps, inside the ship; but it might be that vehicles had already been unloaded and were parked at the base of the ship. It was still too dark to see.

Then Asa reminded us that the Earth would be rising soon, shining like silver and making it almost as clear as day. In fact, a pale glimmer was already showing behind the pointed hills to the north.

'Maybe we should go now,' I suggested. 'If we wait till it gets clear they may spot us.

But Spike was unwilling to leave just yet. 'I'd like to be certain about those jeeps, Jeremy. And they may have other gadgets, too, that it would be useful to know about . . . Say, what's happening now? The soldiers are beginning to move about.'

From our vantage point we watched with interest. First of all a searchlight shone out from the side of the ship, directed downwards and bringing into view the hydraulic landing-gear. Four men swarmed down the ladder to the ground. Then a clanking noise overpowered the hum of the atomic motor and from the open hatch there emerged the arm of a derrick. At the end of it hung a jeep which had apparently been brought up by lift from a lower compartment. There was a shout, and the jeep was slowly lowered until the men at the base of the ship caught and unhooked it.

We settled down, kneeling behind a rock, to see what else would happen; and for nearly half an hour we stayed there, while the enemy unloaded four jeeps and some other cargo which we couldn't distinguish. Spike thought it was food and ammunition, and probably a number of scientific instruments. We did recognise a load of tommy-guns with the rifles.

Then over the horizon appeared a rim of brilliant light.

Asa started. 'Look—the Earth! We must get back to the jeep at once!'

'Yeah.' Spike scrambled to his feet. 'They're just about finished unloading, and in any case we've found out most of what your father and Dr. McKinnon wanted to know. Come on. Try to make as little noise as you can.'

We turned and hurried back up the side of the valley, Asa and I in front, Spike bringing up the rear. The sounds going on in and about the ship began to grow less insistent. As we climbed, however, the Earth rose clear of the hills, spreading a bright glow over everything. Our shadows leaped up in front of us against the steep bank. I began to feel uneasy—naked, somehow. If the enemy looked in our direction now they might just be able to see our shadowy movement.

We were almost three-quarters of the way up when the thing happened. I was climbing a little apart from the others, across a patch of loose rubble. Suddenly the whole mass of stone began to slide beneath my feet. Spike called to me to take care, but by then there was nothing I could do to stop the miniature avalanche. As I slithered back downhill, accompanied by bouncing, rolling rocks, there was a considerable noise, which I realised would almost certainly be heard in the ship. And I was impotent to do anything about it.

I saved myself easily enough by catching hold of a solidly embedded boulder and swinging myself clear on to a patch of turf. But the avalanche continued on its way, rumbling and crashing.

We huddled together, waiting for any sign from the enemy. And as the last echoes of the commotion died away along the valley, it became apparent that Otto Schenk and his men had heard. The sounds of loading stopped abruptly, and the searchlight was jerked upwards until its beam shone steadily on the bank about fifty yards to our left. Then the wavering oblong of light began to move in towards us.

'Get going!' exclaimed Spike. 'Twenty yards farther on it's a lot easier. And if once we get over the ridge up there we can lie low for a while.'

Again we started to climb as fast as we could, slipping and sliding over the rocks and keeping our eyes on the glaring searchlight as it came nearer and nearer. We had done about fifteen yards when it became evident that the light was going to pass right over us. We lay flat against the bank, therefore, breathing fast but keeping as motionless as possible. The beam pinned us down for a moment, bright and uncompromising; and I felt like a dead butterfly in a showcase.

But almost at once it passed away to our right. I had a moment of optimism. Perhaps it wouldn't find us after all. I started up, ready to go on climbing; but Spike's hand clamped hard on my collar.

'Stay still!' he commanded.

The reason became obvious at once. The search-light paused, only a few feet away, then came back. It hovered about us like a gloating hand. Then it steadied, holding us firmly in its brilliance. The enemy had discovered us.

For a moment we continued to lie absolutely still, disappointed and afraid; and that moment was nearly our undoing. The flesh crawled on my back as a sudden shot rang out and then another, and bullets ricochetted viciously on the rocks beside us. In a blinding flash of dismay I realised that Otto Schenk was trying to kill us. Asa caught her breath; but, ignorant of firearms as she was, I'm not sure if she quite understood the danger for another second or two.

'All we can do is make a dash for it,' Spike jerked out. 'Hurry.'

We got to our feet, dazzled by the searchlight, and began to struggle upwards for the ridge. It was a frightening business. Three more rifle-shots came at us, only a few feet away. One of the rock-splinters, indeed, flew up and struck my upper lip, drawing blood which trickled saltily into my mouth. But I paid no heed. Every nerve in my body was taut, concentrated on one end. If only we could reach the ridge before being hit, we ought to find shelter and comparative safety behind it.

The Earth was up now and shining bravely. But the searchlight was so dazzling, and our situation so desperate, that we scarcely noticed its friendly company.

Ten yards now. Five yards.

A bullet buzzed up just at our heels, and then we were past the final barrier of rock and racing across a shoulder of smooth turf. And finally we were over the ridge, out of range of the probing light and safe from the bullets. We lay down, panting, on the moss, thankful for our escape but aware that we had gained only a temporary respite.

Presently we heard the snarl of engines. I crawled to the apex of the ridge and looked over. In the Earthlight I saw eight men piling into two of the enemy jeeps.

Spike spoke at my elbow. 'I thought so. They're coming after us.'

'But they can't come *straight* after us,' whispered Asa. 'Not up that bank.'

'Sure they can't. But they'll go along the floor of the valley for a bit and then come at us from the west.'

Could we get to the jeep in time, before they cut us off? That was the question that came to us all, for we still had four hundred yards to go before we reached the flat plain above the valley. It wasn't a steep climb, and we ought to be able to dodge the searchlight. But the enemy jeeps were moving fast already, and the detour they had to make wasn't particularly long.

We scrambled to our feet, therefore, and began to run again, as fast as we could.

D

CHAPTER XII

The Birds

How we got out of that valley I still don't know. But the enemy must have lost sight of us, for there was no more shooting and eventually the searchlight was switched off.

We got to the flat ground at last, long black shadows cast by the Earth running beside us. Thankfully we raced round behind the knoll and scrambled into the jeep. But just as Spike got the engine going and turned for the long drive back towards the cliff, we saw Otto Schenk's jeeps emerging from the valley far to our right.

They were still half-a-mile away, and barring accidents it seemed to me we had a good chance of reaching the cliff before them. Spike had already brought the speedometer needle up to sixty, and at this rate we should be climbing the rail-track in about forty-five minutes.

But even with our headlamps on the light was a difficult one to drive in, and the shadows were confusing. Besides, so many boulders were concealed among the moss that Spike had to be alert the whole time. Once or twice, indeed, he narrowly missed overgrown jagged rocks which could have broken a spring or perhaps overturned us altogether.

The tyres whined on the dry turf, and we were thrown about as the jeep swerved.

I kept looking back. The enemy jeeps were following us, but as far as I could see they weren't gaining much ground. And after driving for about twenty minutes we began to see the distant black bulk of the cliff against the night sky.

'Do you think they'll come after us up the rail-track?' asked Asa from the rear.

Spike nodded. 'I guess they'll try. But we have those sticks of gelignite. If we reach the top we can blow up the track behind us.'

It was a splendid plan, and I admired Spike for having thought of it. If we could prevent Otto Schenk's men from following us to the top of the cliff they would have to travel hundreds of miles around its base to reach the city.

Then my thoughts of safety were rudely shattered. A bullet cracked into a rock some way to our right, followed at once by the report of a rifle.

'Oh, Spike—they're shooting again!' Asa leaned forward, her fair hair riffling in the wind caused by our speed.

'I expected that,' he answered. 'But they're a long way behind, and it's difficult to aim in a moving jeep.'

There was another shot. It struck fairly wide, twenty yards to the left. I glanced at the speedometer and saw that Spike was now doing sixty-five miles per hour. The bumps weren't too bad, and we were avoiding successfully any uneven ground.

But our pursuers, it seemed, were travelling even

faster. To our dismay the space between us began perceptibly to decrease.

'They're gaining, Spike!' cried Asa. 'They're gaining on us!'

'How much?'

'I—I'm not sure. Can you tell, Jeremy?'

I calculated that they weren't much more than six hundred yards away—maybe less. They were coming in line abreast, swerving and leaping like two buzzing bluebottles, and I knew for certain that at this rate we should never reach the cliff in time. In ten minutes they would catch up with us.

Another shot rang out and the bullet sent up a spurt of dust only a few feet from our near front wheel. On Spike's orders Asa crouched down in the back, while he and I made ourselves as scarce as possible in front. But what worried me most were the tyres. If one of them got hit we should have no chance of escape whatsoever.

'How are we doing?' asked Spike.

'They're still gaining.'

'Newer and faster engines—that's the answer.'

By this time we could see the track in the cliff, slanting diagonally to the top, its surface picked out by the Earthlight and shining like a silver thread. But it was still far off, and the enemy were doggedly closing the gap.

Spike's foot was hard on the accelerator. He was risking an accident now, because if we struck a boulder at such a speed we should be thrown up and over like a shot rabbit. And yet the jeeps behind had already caught up to within a quarter of a mile of us.

'We'll never make it,' I said. 'They're getting closer every minute.'

'Their shooting's more accurate, too,' muttered Spike, as a bullet went *whang* in front of the bonnet. 'I reckon we'll have to depend on a miracle now.'

Our ears were filled by the continuous whine of the jeep's engine. But suddenly an alien sound penetrated my consciousness. It was plaintive, yet somehow pleasant, and instinctively I looked up. Sure enough a great flock of birds was passing over us, a cloud of wings against the shining Earth.

Asa was looking up, too. 'They've come from the city,' she cried. 'My father heard my thoughts and knew we were in danger. He must have sent them.'

'But what good can they do?' I said.

'Don't you understand, Jeremy? There are thousands of them. They'll come down round the jeeps and confuse the drivers, so that they'll be forced to stop.'

We sped on. Our headlamps blazed, but in fact it was almost as clear as day. I craned back to see what was happening and could hardly believe my eyes. The birds swept down on the pursuing jeeps. In the brilliant light their wings covered headlamps and bonnets like a fluttering blanket.

'I wish you could look round, Spike!' There was a surge of excitement and relief in my heart. 'You can't *see* the enemy now. They're completely surrounded. And they've stopped—they've had to stop!'

He kept staring in front, still pushing our vehicle to the utmost. 'I said we'd need a miracle,' he answered, quietly. 'It seems to have happened.'

Then we heard more rifle-shots and realised to our horror that Otto Schenk's men were shooting at the birds. The sound came to us like the crackle of burning twigs. And as we watched—Asa and I— it became evident that the birds had been badly frightened by this attack. Gradually they rose up from about the jeeps like a ragged storm-cloud, leaving the enemy free to come after us again.

But by now we were nearly a mile ahead, and Spike calculated that we could get to the cliff in time. We had, in fact, not much more than two or three miles to go. The birds had successfully done their job and now Asa was sending her thoughts to them, advising them to keep high, out of danger.

A few minutes later we spun hard right at the base of the cliff. Up the narrow track we went, bumping and swaying, with a drop of hundreds of feet on our right-hand side. But we reached the top safely and got out. I grabbed the sticks of gelignite from underneath the rear seat, and Spike and I hurried back down the track.

The enemy jeeps were only half a mile away and heading straight in our direction. The headlights fanned up and down as they curvetted along the rough ground.

We worked fast. Into a hole in the centre of the track—where once the live rail had been embedded —we put two sticks of gelignite, which would be enough to blow a gap six feet wide. Then we tamped them tight with earth and rubble.

Spike struck a match and lit the fuse, and we raced like dervishes for the top of the cliff. Looking back, I saw the enemy turning in towards the cliff.

We flung ourselves down beside Asa, in a little hollow where we had left our jeep. And as we covered our heads with our hands the whole universe seemed to split open in a terrific explosion, much louder than when Spike and I had destroyed the obstruction in the underground river. Small pieces of stone rained down on us and spattered on the bonnet of the jeep like hail.

But presently it was silent again, and we crawled to the edge. A huge hole yawned in the track, making it quite impassable; and far below, at the base of the cliff, the enemy jeeps stood motionless, their crews staring up in amazement and annoyance. One I recognised as Otto Schenk himself.

Spike sighed. 'I guess we've bought a breathing-space. But it's only a breathing-space. Schenk and his men will get to the city sooner or later—round the foot of the cliff.'

We got up and returned to the jeep. As we climbed in the Earth was momentarily blotted out, and the air was filled with sad small cries.

The birds, too, were going home.

CHAPTER XIII

"Surrender—or Resist?"

WHEN WE got back from our patrol Asa and Spike and I found hundreds of people in the tunnel filling small cloth bags with earth. In charge of the work was Petra, Solveg's chief lieutenant; and as soon as we passed in through the doorway he gave instuctions for the great door to be rolled shut and the bags piled high against it on the inside.

At Solveg's house we had a meal, including the drink made from the Apples of Hesikos. While we ate we told Solveg, Uncle Lachlan and Professor Hermanoff about our adventures. Janet and Madge were there, too.

'We were lucky,' Spike said. 'The enemy jeeps had just got to the bottom of the cliff when the charge went off.'

Uncle Lachlan rubbed his chin. 'So before Otto Schenk and his men can reach us here they'll have to make a long detour around the cliff?'

'Yeah, sure.'

'Tell me, Solveg—how far does the cliff extend to the east and west?'

'In your reckoning, Dr. McKinnon, about four hundred miles.'

'I see. That means they can't be here for at least another six hours.' Uncle Lachlan looked thoughtful. 'I should think Otto Schenk will try to get in touch with us before that,' he added. 'By radio.'

There was a small silence. I could feel tension mounting in the cool, airy room, like an approaching heath-fire on a summer's day.

Professor Hermanoff spoke at last. 'And what has to be done in the meantime, Dr. McKinnon?'

'Apart from the door in the tunnel,' said my uncle, 'there are only two ways in which the enemy can possibly get into the city. Schenk will know about them, too, having read Bergman's book and all the newspapers reports. They could come via the underground river, which would mean they'd have to build a raft, and that is most unlikely. Or they could come down the main air-shaft, which would mean miles of rope and tackle and is more unlikely still. At the same time I should suggest guards on both these places.'

'That will be arranged,' said Solveg.

'Thank you, my friend. Then for the next few hours I think we ought to rest as much as we can. Our main task will be to keep a listening-watch on the radio. We can do that in turns, changing every two hours. Hermanoff and I will take the first period. Then Asa and Spike. Then Janet and Jeremy.'

Madge looked anxious. 'Wot about me?' she asked.

'You and the foodmakers must get together. If we

D*

are to withstand a siege, you must have a rationing plan.'

'I see.'

A thought occurred to me. 'What about the ship, Uncle Lachlan? It's standing empty out there, near the mouth of the tunnel. Otto Schenk may try to destroy it.'

'He would find that difficult, I think. The main hatch is locked, and the worst he could do would be to damage the landing-gear with explosives. But if he means to break into the tunnel, he will require all the explosives he's brought with him—if he has sufficient even for that.'

The door opened and Petra came in. His clothes were stained with damp earth, his face rosy with exertion. 'The work is done,' he reported to Solveg. 'The door in the tunnel is closed, and a thousand bags of earth are piled up behind it.'

'Good. Tell the men they may now rest.'

'I will.' Petra paused for a moment, trouble glinting in his blue eyes. 'But I should warn you,' he said, 'they are uneasy. They do not fully understand what is happening.'

'I will give them my thoughts, by means of the Electronome.' Solveg spoke quietly. 'Ask them to remain in their homes until they receive my message.'

'Very well.'

'One thing more. Post sentries in the power-house, in case the enemy try to enter by the underground river—and also at the mouth of the main airshaft.'

'I understand. My own sons will do that.'

As Petra left the room Solveg laid his hand on Uncle Lachlan's arm. 'I am uneasy, too,' he admitted. 'All this is alien to our way of life—this preparation for strife and violence.'

'I know. But violence may be avoided. Schenk may never get farther than the iron door.'

'I hope you are right.'

Uncle Lachlan got briskly to his feet. 'Meanwhile, Spike,' he said, 'I should be obliged if you'd bring the radio in here. Hermanoff and I will begin listening at once.'

Madge hurried off to discuss our supply of rations with the foodmakers. Since our coming to Hesikos they had become her best friends. Her quaint sayings entertained them, I think; and she in her turn was amused by their pleasure in tasting the food she had brought from Earth.

Asa and Janet went to rest in another room, while Spike and I lay down on two couches in the hall. I didn't feel sleepy in the least, after the excitement of the night patrol; but as it happened I did fall into a doze almost at once. Suddenly, I was wide awake again. Solveg's voice—the Voice of Hesikos which we had heard so often before—came echoing into my head. He was giving his thoughts to his people.

My friends, this is a time of crisis. For thousands of years we have lived in peace. But now an enemy comes— an unscrupulous enemy from Earth, whose desire it is to capture our Electronome for his own evil purposes. We are faced with a dilemma—to surrender or to resist. If we surrender, no physical harm will come to us, but our enemy will use the Electronome to bring death and misery to our fellow-beings on Earth. If we resist we shall be in grave physical danger, though Dr. McKinnon, who is our benefactor, believes that by blocking the tunnel we can keep our enemy at bay until winter comes in ten days' time and they will be forced to return to Earth.

We are on the threshold of a new era in Hesikos. Dr. McKinnon has brought tools and machinery and a store of knowledge which will enable us to build new cities and revive our ancient civilisation. What is your answer? Do we surrender and betray our friends? Or do we resist and prove that we have the moral courage to think of others besides ourselves?

The voice in my head became silent. 'Spike—did you hear?' I asked.

'Yeah.' He sat up, leaning on his elbow, and in the dim light his face looked drawn and tired. 'Solveg is a fine man, but his people may turn against him now.'

'How shall we know what they decide? Can we hear *their* thoughts in reply?'

'I dunno. We could, I reckon.'

We waited. The city seemed to be holding its breath. Nothing stirred beneath the great quiet canopy of rock.

Then came the Voice of Hesikos again: *What is your answer? Do we surrender—or resist?*

I tried hard to concentrate; and suddenly, out of a silence, the answer surged up in our minds like the swelling chorus of a song: the answer of the peaceful people of Hesikos roused at last to energy.

We resist! We resist! We resist!

CHAPTER XIV

The Atomic Gun

I SLEPT FOR four hours. Then Spike, who had been on listening-watch with Asa, shook me by the shoulder.

'Come on, kid—your turn. Janet's at the radio next door already.'

'Heard anything from Otto Schenk?'

'Not a whisper.'

And after Janet and I had been listening for over ninety minutes, and our spell was coming to an end, I began to wonder if he meant to call us at all. By that time, even if the jeeps had made a comparatively slow journey round the cliff, he and his men ought to have been fairly close to the mouth of the tunnel.

Janet seemed to have been struck by the same idea. 'D'you think he really will try to get in touch with us, as your uncle says? I mean, he knows now that it's not going to be a tame surrender. But he has plenty of arms and ammunition, and we have none. Why should he bother to speak to us again?'

'I think Uncle Lachlan believes he'd rather try to frighten us than use force.'

'Maybe so. But—oh, Jeremy, I hate all this! Somehow Hesikos was always so happy and peaceful before. Now there's this waiting—this tension. I'm sorry for Solveg and his people.'

'So am I. But if they stick it out and we beat Otto Schenk, they'll be far *tougher* than they were.'

'Yes—and much better able to face difficulties in the future. That's quite true.'

Madge came in, rather anxious, to find out if there had been news.

'None at all,' said Janet. 'How have you been getting on yourself?'

'Oh, I've 'ad a wonderful time. The cooks showed me 'ow to make these little 'oney-cakes. Delicious!'

'Are there plenty of rations?' I asked.

'Nothing to worry about there, Jeremy. We could 'old out for weeks. Not on the tins we brought, of course. But the foodmakers 'ere 'ave great stores of stuff 'idden away—flour and 'oney and fruit—all kinds of things. I'll 'ave to take a few of their recipes back to Inverard with me.'

Janet fiddled with her pencil. 'If we ever do get back to Inverard,' she said, quietly.

'Oh, keep yore pecker up!' Madge smiled and patted her shoulder. 'We'll get back all right. There's just one thing that worries me,' she went on. ' 'Ow do these characters 'ere all speak English?'

I told her they didn't speak at all, and her eyes widened in disbelief. 'Oh, come off it, Jeremy! They were chattering away sixteen to the dozen down there in the store.'

'Jeremy's right,' said Janet. 'They don't actually *speak*. Solveg explained it the last time we were here. They simply transfer thoughts to our minds. Thoughts have no specific language, you see; and as we receive them from the people of Hesikos we unconsciously translate them into English.'

'Well, if you say so, Janet. But I can 'ear them —and they seem to 'ear me, too, when I talk.'

'Solveg says it's a mental illusion. With the Hesikians it works in reverse. They know we're making sounds, but they disregard that and concentrate on receiving the ideas behind our words.' She broke off as a crackle came from the loudspeaker. 'I say—what's this? Turn up the volume, Jeremy.'

I did so; and almost as soon as I touched the control the voice came through: 'Here is Otto Schenk. Are you receiving me? Over.'

'We must get Dr. McKinnon,' said Janet, quickly.

Madge got up. 'I'll tell 'im. 'E was sleeping like a baby in the 'all when I came through.'

She had scarcely left the room when our enemy spoke again: 'Here is Otto Schenk. Are you receiving me? Over.' There was no distortion, which meant that he wasn't far away.

Then Uncle Lachlan was with us, rubbing his eyes. But when Schenk called for a third time his chin stuck out and he switched over to transmission with energy and decision: 'McKinnon calling Otto Schenk. Receiving you loud and distinct. Over.'

'Otto Schenk calling McKinnon. We have found the door of the tunnel closed and suspect a barrier behind it. You are being foolish. You cannot keep us out. We are equipped with an atomic gun which will destroy any barrier. Better to avoid violence and let us have the Electronome now. Over.'

'Is he bluffing?' I asked.

Uncle Lachlan shook his head. 'I don't know. I just don't know.' He pressed the transmission key. 'McKinnon calling Otto Schenk. Break into the city if you can. You have only ten days in which to do it. Then you will perish in the cold outside. Over.'

'Here is Otto Schenk.' The voice was sharper now and edged with anger. 'You are a fool, Dr. McKinnon. And a fool must pay for his folly. Over and out.'

The loudspeaker went dead and I switched off.

After a moment Janet said: 'An atomic gun— what does he mean by that?'

'Such an invention does exist.' Uncle Lachlan frowned, clasping and unclasping his hands between his knees. 'It fires atomic particles into a metal obstruction and eventually destroys it in much the same way as an oxy-acetylene burner.'

'In that case,' I said, 'the iron door won't be much good.'

'It depends, Jeremy. And as you suggest, Schenk *may* be bluffing. If he's not bluffing, however—if he has got an atomic gun—there's always the possibility that it's less effective than he tries to make out. That door is very thick. An ordinary burner would take days to cut it open. After that there are the bags of earth, and I reckon we could build them up even faster than he could work a way in.'

Janet jabbed the point of her pencil on the writing-pad. 'Ten days,' she said, 'is a long time to hold out.'

'It can be done. Nothing's impossible. And new ideas may occur to Solveg and Hermanoff.' Uncle Lachlan got quickly to his feet. 'Now I'd better go and give them the news. Afterwards we'll visit the tunnel and try to find out if Schenk has begun work on the other side of the barrier.'

I told him I thought Madge was bringing some coffee.

'Right,' he said. 'Tell her we should all appreciate a cup. I'll be back with Solveg and the Professor in a couple of minutes.'

As we drank our coffee and nibbled some honey-cakes, nobody said very much. I remembered the mood of Hesikos on our first two visits—serene and peaceful and happy. And we had been happy, too. But now the mood had changed. There was fear in the minds of the people of Hesikos, and it affected us all, making us jumpy and nervous—though of course we did our best to hide it.

Uncle Lachlan became irritable, as he so often was on Earth. He put down his cup and saucer with a clatter. 'Sitting here won't do us much good!' he exclaimed. 'I'm going up to the tunnel to find out what's happening. Who's coming with me? Hermanoff?'

'Yes, I will come.'

'Spike?'

'I reckon there's not much else to do.'

I said I'd like to go as well.

'Right, Jeremy. What about the ladies?'

Asa explained that she and Madge and Janet had decided to help in making cloth bags, in case more were needed for the barrier. The supply had run out, and the clothmakers had asked for as many volunteer assistants as possible.

'Good,' said Uncle Lachlan. 'What about you, Solveg?'

The old man was sitting by himself, his chin resting on his hands. 'Something has occurred to me,' he answered, quietly. 'I seem to remember that long centuries ago Hesikos was invaded by enemies from another planet, and that the ruler of the time took desperate action against them. Somewhere in our library there is a book which describes what he did. I must find that book, for its story may guide us now.'

Uncle Lachlan became more irritable than ever. 'What happened in the past won't help us! We are more concerned with the future.'

'The past is always the foundation on which the future is built,' returned Solveg, with calm patience. 'History and science go hand in hand.'

'Tcha! Words, my friend—empty words! You'd be better employed chasing up your men to fill more bags of earth!'

'Petra will see to that, Dr. McKinnon.'

His dignity cooled my uncle's temper. 'Sorry!' he said. 'I didn't mean to be critical. My nerves are a bit on edge.'

We got into the jeep—Professor Hermanoff, Spike, Uncle Lachlan and I. It took us only about five minutes to speed through the city, pass out by the main gate and enter the upward-sloping tunnel. The place was softly lit, probably by a kind of concealed strip-lighting reflected from the roof as in the city itself. In the rough-hewn walls specks of iridonium shone like cats' eyes; and the memory returned to me of my excitement when Professor Bergman discovered that iridonium mixed with lead would produce gold and of my astonishment when Professor Hermanoff explained that the catalyst was common salt. It all seemed to have happened a long, long time ago. Even my disappointment when it was proved that iridonium couldn't survive the journey to Earth now seemed shadowy and vague, and somehow unimportant. We had learned many things on Hesikos since then. But—I wondered— had we learned properly how to deal with Otto Schenk?

Spike drove round a quick bend and we came in sight of the great mound of chocolate-coloured bags heaped high to the roof. Thirty or forty feet behind the pile was the iron door. And beyond that the enemy.

Petra was standing guard by himself while the men rested. As the jeep stopped he came forward to greet us.

'Any news?' inquired my uncle.

'None. For the past six hours, ever since the barrier was completed, there has been silence.'

'Your sons are on watch at the air-shaft and in the power-house?'

'Yes. But they won't be disturbed. The enemy are here—beyond the door. Their thoughts come to me, hard and eager, as they prepare to break in.'

'Are you afraid?'

'I am afraid,' he said. 'In Hesikos we have always known what to expect. Now it is different.'

Spike put an arm about his shoulders. 'Keep your chin up, Petra! It takes a big man to admit he's afraid. . .'

It was very quiet. If Otto Schenk began using his atomic gun we should hear it quite plainly. According to Uncle Lachlan, it worked in a series of short explosions. These would be muffled by the barrier, but the vibrations would come to us along the stone floor.

'Dr. McKinnon,' said Hermanoff, presently, 'I have no knowledge of this atomic gun. Is it used as a kind of drill, making a pattern of small holes and then cutting between them?'

'That's the idea, more or less. In a thick metal door like the one out there it may take anything up to ten shots to cut a single small hole.'

'At that rate,' said Spike, 'Schenk will take a long time to break in.'

'That's been my opinion all along. If he gets through the door, of course, his progress may be more rapid, but I hope we can repair the barrier faster than his men can clear it away.'

We stood there talking. The air was fresh, swirling down from the hill outside through the ventilator-shafts. But my hands were warm and sticky, and there was a sense of oppression about the tunnel which daunted us all.

Suddenly we heard it—a muffled explosion behind the barrier. It was followed by another and yet another in quick succession. The ground trembled beneath our feet.

I looked at Uncle Lachlan. His face was hard

'It's started,' he said.

CHAPTER XV

The City is Besieged

FOR SOME time we listened to the muffled explosions beyond the barrier, as Otto Schenk began his assault on the iron door. At each burst of sound the whole tunnel shook, and in my mind's eye I could see holes being punched deeper and deeper into the thick metal.

'The atomic gun is more powerful than I thought,' said Uncle Lachlan, presently. 'But the door is strong. We still have a breathing space. Petra——'

'Yes?'

'Spike will take you back to the city in the jeep. Collect your workmen again. We must put more bags of earth into the tunnel. A hundred men if they are available.'

'Very well, Dr. McKinnon.'

'Professor Hermanoff and Jeremy and I will remain here to note developments.'

On and on they went, those quick reverberating reports, until at last they beat against our ears with a painful physical effect. Something inside me shrank and cowered away.

Hours went by, and Petra and his men built up more bags of earth. Everyone remained outwardly calm, but you could feel the tension growing.

Almost as distinctly as if I was there, I could see Otto Schenk, crouched outside the door, taking his turn at operating the gun.

Towards the end of the second day Uncle Lachlan and I were in Solveg's house, with the radio turned on.

'How much longer do you think the door will stand?' I asked.

'I don't know. But it's proving a harder nut than Schenk expected. I think he'll try to get in touch with us again.'

'Isn't there anything we can do? I mean, if some of us climbed out by an air-shaft and tried to take them by surprise——'

'Quite impracticable!' he said. 'They won't be caught napping. If only we had a few rifles!'

'Solveg doesn't seem to have any ideas, either.'

'No. He spends his time in that library of his, looking for some ancient book. I don't know what he expects to find in it. Some secret of his ancestors, he says. If there's one thing I can't stand, Jeremy, it's inaction!'

'The people of Hesikos are braver than I thought they'd be.'

'I know. But do they fully realise the wickedness of Otto Schenk? Madge is the same. She puts her trust in the ultimate goodness of things—but that doesn't always work out. Not without sacrifice of some kind.'

We sat there for a long time, waiting for something to happen. It was an instinct—a kind of second-sight which warned us that our enemy was thinking about getting in touch with us. And sure enough it proved true in the end. There was a crackle on the loudspeaker, and the smooth, dislikable voice came through.

'Here is Otto Schenk. Are you receiving me? Over.'

Uncle Lachlan snatched up the mike. 'McKinnon calling Otto Schenk. Receiving you loud and clear. Over.'

'Otto Schenk calling McKinnon. Soon now the door will be destroyed. You have no chance against us, but to save further trouble I have a proposal to make. Over.'

'He's weakening!' I blurted out.

'I wonder?' Uncle Lachlan didn't sound too confident. He pressed the transmitting switch and spoke again: 'McKinnon calling Otto Schenk. Let's hear your proposal. Over.'

'Otto Schenk calling McKinnon. You are one of the greatest scientists in the world. I am one of the richest men. Together we could dictate our terms to the human race. Let us join forces. Let us brush aside the people of Hesikos and take the Electronome between us. What is your answer? Over.'

There was a momentary pause, and a text came into my head—one that I had learned at school: 'All this power I will give thee . . . if thou therefore wilt worship me.' Then Uncle Lachlan was saying quietly: 'Well, Jeremy, what would your answer be?'

'I'd tell him nothing doing.'

The transmitting key clicked over. 'McKinnon

calling Otto Schenk. The answer is no. Now and always. Over and out.'

He switched off and leaned back on the couch, grim-faced and pale.

'Why did he make an offer like that?' I said. 'D'you think the door's too thick for his atomic gun after all?'

'No. He'll break it down all right.' Uncle Lachlan spoke with deliberation. 'He may be afraid of his reception, though—once he does get in.'

'How d'you mean?'

'He realises that the people of Hesikos are expert scientists. For all he knows they may possess a secret answer to his rifles and tommy-guns.'

'But they don't, actually.'

'So it appears. But Schenk hasn't discovered that yet. He'll be still more uncertain, now that we've turned his offer down. If he can wage a war of nerves, so can we!'

But I remembered that eight days still remained before winter would come. . .

Two of those days passed.

Three days.

Four days. . .

There was silence in the city, but the sharp explosions continued, slowly destroying the door. Sometimes they would stop, and we would wonder if Schenk had given up. Then they'd start again, as strong and vicious as ever.

None of us slept a great deal, though we took turns at lying down and resting at regular intervals. Asa was wonderfully good-humoured, and her

example did much to keep up the spirits of the
Hesikians, to whom such a strain was new and
unexpected. Her father was quiet, but there was a
surprising lack of apprehension in his attitude.
He seemed resigned to whatever might occur and
ready to meet danger when it really arrived.

Uncle Lachlan fretted, restlessly moving about
between the city and the tunnel and exhorting
Petra and the workmen to greater efforts. Spike
and Janet and I helped to strengthen the barrier,
and when we weren't working mingled with the
people, doing our best to maintain their morale.
Madge spent most of her time with the foodmakers.
As they doled out our rations, carefully measuring
the quantities, they were probably the most cheerful persons in the whole community.

On the morning of the fifth day Uncle Lachlan
and Solveg and I were in the tunnel, listening.
The explosions had been going on intermittently
throughout the morning; but suddenly there came
a longer pause than usual.

'They've stopped,' I said, not quite knowing
what to think.

Solveg nodded. 'They are almost through. The
metal of the door is being cooled with water before
they make a final effort.'

'How do you know?' asked Uncle Lachlan.

'I can read their thoughts. They are full of
triumph, for very soon they will only have the earth
barrier to deal with.'

My uncle stood rigid and quiet. 'So it's come
to that!' he murmured.

I shivered. But there was a certain amount of comfort in the thought that even though the enemy did break through they'd still take a long time shifting the bags behind the door.

Ten minutes passed. The tunnel was silent, and the barrier looked solid and safe. But all at once there was another burst from the atomic gun, followed by a clang of metal. The door was down.

Uncle Lachlan pondered, slowly rubbing his chin with his knuckles. 'The gun won't be of much use against soft earth,' he said, 'and if they're forced to remove the bags with their hands we still have a chance. But it has occurred to me—they may use ordinary explosives now, if they've brought any. By such means they could blast a way in comparatively quickly.'

'Faster than we could build up more bags?'

'Much faster, Jeremy. But they may not have reckoned with a barrier of earth.'

Solveg was standing by the bonnet of the jeep, apparently lost in thought. Presently, however, he looked up, a frown on his high forehead. 'I cannot read their minds any more,' he said. 'Everything has become confused. But I have a feeling, Dr. McKinnon, that nothing will stop them now. Nothing physical at least.'

'Nothing physical? How else can we stop them?'

'There is only one way that I can see. The way taken by a ruler of Hesikos long ago, when invaders from another planet threatened to destroy our people. Yesterday I found the book telling what he did.'

I was about to ask a question when the tunnel rocked to a louder, more diffused explosion. This time it wasn't caused by the atomic gun.

'Then they do have explosives!' I exclaimed.

'Looks like it,' replied Uncle Lachlan. 'They'll take half an hour at least to clear away the debris and set each charge, but three more blasts like that will clear the whole tunnel.'

'Couldn't we *try* more bags of earth?'

'No good. It would only postpone the result for a few hours. And winter isn't due for another five days.'

'Evil will come to us,' said Solveg, quietly. 'We cannot prevent it now. But we can still defeat it.'

My uncle glanced up. 'You talk in riddles!' he said. 'What exactly do you mean?'

But the old man was unwilling to go further. 'Let us return to the city,' he answered. 'I will tell you —later.'

And in fact there wasn't much point in staying in the tunnel. As the explosions came closer we should be able to hear them distinctly in the central square. Besides, Solveg wanted to speak to his people— to tell them to be calm and to remain indoors. We got into the jeep, therefore, and Uncle Lachlan drove us back.

About an hour later, on the request of Solveg, we gathered in the small building which housed the Electronome—Solveg himself and Asa, Uncle Lachlan and Professor Hermanoff, Madge and Janet and Spike and I. From the open door we could see part of the gate of the city right up to the tunnel.

No one moved in the streets. We had heard two more explosions, each nearer than the one before; and now we were waiting for a third, which would probably be the last before Schenk and his men emerged from the tunnel.

My mouth was dry and sticky, and even Uncle Lachlan seemed to have lost his air of craggy defiance. It was Solveg who gave an impression of confidence. Spike moved about in a nervous way, looking at his watch.

'It's time—and past time!' he exclaimed, suddenly. 'Thirty-one minutes since the last explosion. Why the heck doesn't the next one come?'

Asa put a hand on his arm. 'Please—we must be calm!'

'How can I be calm?' he shot back at her. 'We're so darned helpless, waiting here! Waiting, waiting. . .'

'I know 'ow you feel, Mr. Stranahan.' Madge was tense and even a little pale. 'Why can't we go out and fight them with our bare 'ands?'

'Yeah—why not! I——'

'It would be quite useless,' interrupted Professor Hermanoff. 'Schenk and his men are fully armed. We should be killed like animals.'

Spike hunched a shoulder at him. 'Better to be killed like animals than to stay here and do nothing!'

Uncle Lachlan was standing with Solveg near the railing in front of the Electronome. 'You must tell me—what is your plan?' he said, abruptly. 'You say you have a plan to defeat the enemy——'

'Patience, my friend.' The old man was actually

able to smile. 'Let us wait and see if it will be necessary.'

A minute passed. And another. And yet another.

'Jeremy,' said Janet, quietly, 'do you remember —the time-bomb in the ship?'

'Yes.'

'This is much the same, isn't it?'

'Something the same. Only—only worse, I think. We should have died quickly if the bomb had gone off. But now we don't know what Otto Schenk will do.'

Spike passed us on restless feet. 'The half hour's up long ago. Nearly thirty-four minutes now——'

Then we heard it—a dull, rumbling crash. We crowded to the door. Out of the mouth of the tunnel—far away beyond the city gate—came flying a cloud of earth and rubble. It appeared that the enemy had finished the job.

We waited for the dust to settle; and suddenly, like ghostly figures in a sea fog, we saw them coming —Otto Schenk in front carrying a metal cylinder which was probably the atomic gun, and behind him, armed with tommy-guns, eight soldiers in their dark shirts and trousers and high leather boots.

For a time no one said a word. Then Uncle Lachlan burst out: 'Solveg, they'll be at the gate in less than five minutes. What have you in mind? Or have you anything in mind at all?'

'I will tell you, Dr. McKinnon.' There was something about him—an air of solemn authority, perhaps—which made us all turn and listen. 'Thirty thousand years ago a strange ship arrived here from outer space. Which world it came from I do not know. It may have been Mars or Venus—or another asteroid. But inside the ship were creatures of an alien kind, four-legged and hideous, but with sharp, intelligent minds which our people could read. They besieged the city and broke open the door in the tunnel and came amongst us, intent on stealing anything of value they could find. Then they set covetous eyes on the Electronome. But the ruler of that time—Kerin was his name—decided to treble the power of the Electronome. He touched the white lever—there at the side of the machine— and more and more electricity streamed up from the power-house until the wires turned red. Then Kerin put his hands on the terminals and directed his thoughts into the minds of the invaders. And the invaders were seized by a sudden terror, and they fled from the city and re-embarked in their ship, never to be seen again.'

'You believe this to be true?' asked Uncle Lachlan.

Solveg nodded. His eyes were bright, yet seemingly focused on something far away. 'It is written in the ancient book. The storyteller was Kerin's son, who became ruler in his father's place.'

'Can *you* do what Kerin did?'

'I can—and will. There is power in the Electronome, even when it is only lightly charged with electricity. You have felt it, all of you. When that charge is trebled, there is no limit to what it may accomplish.'

Spike, listening intently, caught the old man's

arm. 'But Solveg—surely there's a snag? You have to operate the machine. If the power is trebled won't you be in danger?'

It was Asa who answered, quiet and intent. 'My father hasn't told you the end of the story. Kerin saved our people and put the invaders to flight. But he died in doing it.'

E

CHAPTER XVI

Power

OTTO SCHENK and his soldiers were at the gate. They swung in, marching in file, and began to approach our position by way of the main street. They would be on us in a few minutes.

'Solveg—is this true?' exclaimed my uncle. 'Did Kerin die?'

'Yes. But that was long ago. We have learned much about the Electronome since then and are better able to resist its power.'

Spike jerked out: 'Dr. McKinnon, say the word! We'll go out there and stop them ourselves!'

But Solveg restrained him. 'I will stop them,' he promised. He turned to Asa. 'Have you told Dorman in the power-house to expect a heavy load?'

'Yes, Father.'

My uncle made a protest. 'Solveg, you can't *do* it! I——'

'There is nothing else to be done.' The old man went under the railing towards the machine, and for a moment I was conscious only of the quiet *tr-r-r-rick* of its scanning beam. Then he turned and faced us. 'My friends, I must warn you—when I press this lever the gentle note of the Electronome will change. It will rise to such a pitch that it will almost vanish. Then, as I take hold of the terminals, your ears will catch distant sounds, and you will know my thoughts and the thoughts of our enemies. But for you there will be no danger. The power will be flowing through my body.'

Distantly now, in the silent city, I could hear the tramp of feet. But I paid no attention to the advance of the enemy. I was watching Solveg.

He pressed the white lever. Slowly at first, then faster and faster, the sound of the Electronome became a high twanging wail. It was like ethereal music, rising and falling in a rhythmical cadence. But at last, as Solveg grasped the terminals and stood stiff and rigid by the machine, this faded and disappeared. Out of a vast echoing distance there came into our heads the *crump* of marching feet. It was like a close-up: a close-up of Otto Schenk and his men, which translated into words the very nature of their thoughts.

Solveg's face was as white as death, but he stood firm and steady, holding the terminals; and all at once, though his lips were motionless, I heard his voice. It, too, came out of an echoing distance, cutting across the trample of the marching feet.

'Stop, Otto Schenk! Stop!'

The heavy footsteps hesitated, faltered and came to a halt. Out of the hollow distance came the voice of our enemy: 'Who is that? Who is speaking?' And a murmur from his soldiers: 'Herr Schenk, we are afraid!'

It was a picture in sound, conjured up by the power of the Electronome. We couldn't see the enemy, who were still a few hundred yards distant down the main street; nevertheless, it seemed as if they were in the building beside us. I even caught the frightened irritation in Schenk's mind as he blurted out: 'Afraid! I am afraid of nothing! March on!'

Again the marching feet. Again the voice of Solveg: 'Stop, Otto Schenk! Stop!'

Once more the enemy halted. There was silence, except for the throbbing echo of the Electronome. Then a whisper came from Otto Schenk: 'A mist is floating before my eyes. I cannot see . . . Whose voice is that?'

'It is the Voice of Hesikos—the Voice of Power which can destroy all evil.'

But Schenk was mentally strong. His mind still fought against the influence of Solveg. 'It is a trick!' he cried. 'Come on, you fools! Come on!'

'No, Herr Schenk! Let us go back!'

'Come on, I said——'

'But darkness is on us. We cannot move. . .'

Solveg's voice grew louder. 'Go back, Otto Schenk! Go back to your ship and return to Earth, or the power of Hesikos will engulf your mind and body, and that will be the end.'

Schenk was stammering now: 'I—I do not understand. I cannot think!'

For a moment Solveg swayed. I saw his face grow whiter still. This was how his ancestor Kerin had repelled the invaders, only to be killed himself by the power of the machine. Would Solveg die, too? That was the terrible thought which formed a background to the echoing voices in my head. A telepathic battle was being waged around us. Would the result be triumph—or tragedy?

One of the soldiers cried out: 'There is death in the city, Herr Schenk! We must go!'

'And so abandon all my plans?' He was struggling hard, but into his voice had come a timbre of helplessness.

Then Solveg rallied and spoke again. 'The Electronome is not for you, Otto Schenk. It is an instrument for good, not for evil. Go back! Go back!'

And suddenly I knew that whatever the cost might be, Solveg had won. Schenk's bluster faded like a summer breeze. 'I am finished!' he muttered. 'I cannot fight any more,' And into my head came the sound of shuffling footsteps, moving away.

I turned from Solveg. Far down, near the gate, I saw the enemy in retreat, stumbling like blinded men towards the tunnel.

'It's like what happened thousands of years ago!' exulted Spike. 'They're scared out of their wits!'

All at once, as Otto Schenk and his men disappeared, I became aware that the twanging, echoing sound was no longer pulsing through my head. In the building there was complete silence. Even the quiet *tr-r-r-rick* of the scanning beam was missing. The same idea must have occurred to everybody, for we all turned together. With a feeling of sick apprehension I saw that Solveg had fallen. He lay slumped across the machine, his white tunic spread like a tablecloth on the transparent mica cover.

Asa ran to him. 'Father—what has happened?' she cried. But there was no answer.

We gathered at the railing, and I saw that the flowing wires in the Electronome were now dull and dead. Spike and I were about to go closer; but Uncle Lachlan ordered us to stay where we were.

Asa knelt down, chafing the heavily veined hands which still clasped the terminals in a rigid grip. She was whispering and pleading, trying to make her father hear. But as far as I could see there was no spark of life in his body.

'Asa,' said Uncle Lachlan, suddenly, 'do you remember when Jeremy and Spike lost consciousness, last time we were here, Solveg healed them with his hands? Can't *you* heal *him*?'

She seemed to pull herself together. 'I will try, Dr. McKinnon.'

'Would it not be better to remove his hands from the terminals?' suggested Professor Hermanoff.

'No. The touch of the machine may help.' Uncle Lachlan had regained his gruff authority. 'At this moment Solveg and it are one. If contact were broken he might never recover. But we can reduce the power.' He leaned forward across the railing, risking his own safety rather than ours, and thrust the white lever down to its original position.

'You mean, they may come to life again together, the man and the machine?'

'Yes.'

Asa's slim sensitive fingers were soothing the swollen veins. 'Father,' she whispered, 'come back! Come back!'

I stood beside Madge. I felt sure he was dead, and said so; but she put her hand on my shoulder. 'Wait, Jeremy. There's something 'ere you and I don't understand.'

Uncle Lachlan was leaning against the rail, his eyes intent. Suddenly he said: 'I may be wrong, Hermanoff, but I have the impression that life still lingers in those wires. A suggestion merely— a flickering spark.'

I stared at the wires beneath the transparent cover. They all looked dead, except that on one occasion what might have been a shimmer ran through them. But I wondered if that wasn't a trick of the light.

'If there *is* life in the machine,' said Hermanoff, 'do you think Solveg may be alive, too?'

'Yes. But we shall soon know. If the Electronome resumes its gentle ticking there will be hope for him.'

Time passed. Asa's fingers moved across the broad pale forehead; but her father continued to lie there, stricken and silent.

And then I nearly jumped out of my skin. For an instant the wires glowed, followed by a *tr-r-r-rick* from the scanning beam: an almost imperceptible sound, but one which unmistakably promised life.

'Dr. McKinnon,' said Asa, 'my father moved!'

'Keep your hands on his forehead. Keep calling him!' he answered.

We held our breaths and waited. The seconds ticked past, and I was beginning to wonder if after all our hopes were to be disappointed, when suddenly the wires glowed again, and for the space of about ten seconds the scanning beam made its quiet sound.

Then the wires dulled down and remained dull for another minute. Finally, however, life returned to them once more, and this time it didn't die away. And as the machine maintained its lively pulse I saw a film of moisture appear on the mica beneath Solveg's mouth. I saw him stir and move restlessly.

Then his eyes were open. 'Where am I?' he asked. 'What has happened?'

Asa was trembling with relief and happiness. She held him in her arms and said: 'Oh, Father— you are alive. That's all that matters.'

'Have I been asleep?'

Uncle Lachlan explained. 'It was the machine, Solveg. The power overcame you.'

'The machine?' Slowly his eyes brightened, as memory came back to him. 'A velvet darkness fell upon my mind, and my body seemed to be sinking into nothingness. But I remember now! Otto Schenk! Otto Schenk and his armed men——'

Asa broke in quietly. 'It's all right, Father. They've gone,' she said.

'Your plan was successful,' my uncle told him. 'Like the invaders of long ago they were seized by a sudden great terror.'

'I am glad.' Waveringly Solveg smiled. 'Would you say that I have repaid our debt, Dr. McKinnon, to you and all our friends from Earth?'

'You have. More than repaid it.'

It was arranged that Uncle Lachlan, Professor Hermanoff, Spike and I should take him back to his house. As we passed out by the door, gently carrying our burden, I heard Madge's voice: 'Poor old gentleman—'e deserves a rest!'

CHAPTER XVII

Goodbye to Hesikos

THAT NIGHT Uncle Lachlan and Spike and I took the jeep and went back to the ship. It was just as we had left it; and the first thing we did was to turn on the radar, which was beamed on the enemy ship.

As the long continuous flashes appeared on the screen we realised that it was still on the ground where it had landed, a hundred miles away. This was not surprising, however, as it was only eight hours since Otto Schenk and his men had left the city. Their journey back, around the flank of the great cliff, would have taken six hours at least. And another two hours would probably be required for loading up.

At the same time a small misgiving stuck like a burr in my thoughts. 'Is there a chance that Otto Schenk will change his mind?' I asked. 'I mean, is he likely to come back and try again?'

Uncle Lachlan shook his head. 'The influence of the Electronome—or of Hesikos, rather—will be with him all his life, I think.'

'I guess you're right, Dr. McKinnon.' Spike carefully adjusted the controls. 'He may be a different character altogether when he gets back to Earth.'

Ten minutes later a change came over the radar. The long flashes were broken up into instantaneous points of light, occurring once every second or so, which indicated that the enemy ship had taken off. We watched as it climbed farther and farther away from Hesikos, until in the end its progress could no longer be followed on the screen.

After a time Spike said: 'We'll soon have to be going, too, I reckon?'

'The day after tomorrow,' replied Uncle Lachlan. 'We'll unload the tools and machinery straight away. Petra and his men are coming to help in the morning.'

Spike thought that this had been the strangest of all our visits. 'What *is* the power in the Electronome?' he said.

Uncle Lachlan put down the notebook in which he had been roughing out a plan for the unloading. 'That's a secret I very much doubt if we shall ever discover. Sometimes I think I have found the answer: a fusion of mind and matter caused by electricity. Then I find myself as much in the dark as before. It's like trying to sort out the details of a dream.'

'In some ways the people of Hesikos are so like us,' I said. 'In others they're quite different.'

'I know what you mean, Jeremy. I wonder what Otto Schenk thinks about it all? When I remember how arrogant he was, and the humiliation he had to suffer, I can feel almost sorry for him.'

The scientists of Hesikos were pleased and excited about the stuff we had brought. Under Professor

Hermanoff's guidance they had already begun to build an atomic pile, and they were looking forward to the years ahead, when Hesikos would recover its lost civilisation and great cities would spread over the planet.

But after the unloading had been completed the following morning we had only a few hours in which to share their excitement. The cold of winter was due in another three days, and it was time we were leaving. Solveg, now fully recovered, invited us to take a final meal in his house. Then we visited the power-house and the dell where the birds and animals lived. And as a parting gift we each received a roll of film from the library of ancient records. Madge had acquired an additional gift from the foodmakers—a long list of detailed Hesikian recipes.

As we left the city the people waved to us, and I could feel their thoughts, eager that we should hasten back. Then we sped up through the long tunnel, still strewn with debris after Otto Schenk's assault. It was a beautiful day outside, warm and sunny as always, but when I looked towards the north I could see small fingers of ice beginning to form on the peaks of the distant hills; and everywhere the petals of the little white flower were beginning to curl inwards.

Solveg and Asa came with us to the ship. At the foot of the long ladder they said goodbye to Janet and Madge, Spike and Professor Hermanoff. Finally only my uncle and I were left with them.

'Saying goodbye is a thing I hate,' growled Uncle Lachlan. 'Au revoir is better.'

Asa smiled and nodded. 'Au revoir is certainly better. You and Jeremy will come back.'

'You bet,' I said. 'In a year or two—maybe sooner.'

'I wonder!'

It was Solveg who spoke, with an oddly serious expression. Even Asa was surprised; and Uncle Lachlan, blunt as usual, demanded what he meant.

'Today,' he answered, slowly, 'our astronomers discovered a strange thing. You remember on your last visit I told you how in the distant past our people reached a stage of civilisation similar to yours on Earth today, and how the explosion of an atomic bomb altered the course of Hesikos through space, so that our climate changed and life was almost completely destroyed?'

'I remember. It was then that you outlawed explosives of all kinds and refused to face the problem of evil.'

'Yes, Dr. McKinnon. But *you* taught us how to face it—as face it we must in the future. I followed your teaching two days ago, when the enemy entered the city—and as the Electronome became silent it seems that our planet shook a little and began to move back towards the sun.'

'Father,' exclaimed Asa, 'you didn't tell me!'

'I concealed my thoughts until I could work out the delicate calculations for myself.'

Uncle Lachlan rubbed his chin. 'You mean Hesikos is now travelling *away* from the Earth?'

'Yes—at the rate of hundreds of miles each minute.

And as the months and the years go on that rate will steadily increase.'

'Then your climate will become warm again? You will be able to live on the surface?'

'That is true.'

'And soon,' I said, 'you'll be so far away that a journey from the Earth will take years instead of days?'

'My boy, I speak only for the present and the immediate future. In centuries to come Hesikos will circle back towards the Earth. But you and your uncle and Asa and I—I think we shall never meet again.'

'Then it really is goodbye,' said Uncle Lachlan.

'Goodbye—in a physical sense,' returned Solveg, with the faraway look in his eyes which I shall always remember. 'But our thoughts will travel through space, and in moments of doubt or anxiety each may help the other.'

We shook hands.

Asa's lips were trembling. 'Jeremy,' she said, 'you won't forget?'

'I won't forget,' I promised. 'Goodbye, Asa.'

'Goodbye. Safe journey—and be happy!'

Solveg put his hands on Uncle Lachlan's shoulders. 'Asa tells me that in your garden at Inverard the flower of Charity grows and multiplies?'

'Indeed it does.'

'Then tend it well—as a memory of Hesikos.'

We turned and began to climb the ladder, with the scent of Hesikos strong and sweet about us. Each step was an effort, but I didn't look back. It would have been a bad thing if Solveg and Asa had discovered that tears were streaming down my cheeks.

CHAPTER XVIII

Trapped in Space

THE MAIN hatch rolled shut. It was almost three minutes to twelve.

'Air-pressure normal?' inquired Uncle Lachlan.

'Yeah—all secure,' said Spike.

'Well, you know the drill,' my uncle continued, as we fastened our safety-belts. 'Slow climb at first, then a speed of fifteen miles per second as we reach the stratosphere. The usual black-out. Then we wake up to find that the rotatory jets have come into action, giving us artificial gravity. There will be complete silence, except for the hum of the motor. The sound of the jets will be left behind. Everybody happy?'

Madge made a wry mouth. 'I wouldn't say '*appy*, Dr. McKinnon!'

We couldn't help laughing, and I began to feel better.

Professor Hermanoff was looking round with interest. 'This is a much bigger ship than I have been used to, Dr. McKinnon. But the system of propulsion is the same, I suppose?'

'Yes. Atomic motor and six main jets. Propellant fuel—plain water, atomically charged.' He broke off. 'One minute to twelve,' he said, abruptly. 'Stand by, Spike.'

'Okay.'

Janet whispered: 'All right, Jeremy?'

'I'm all right,' I said.

'Brace yourselves,' Uncle Lachlan warned us. 'We always lift more violently from Hesikos, on account of the weaker gravity and thinner atmosphere.' He looked at the clock. 'We have exactly ten seconds from now,' he said. 'Nine . . . eight . . . seven . . . six . . . five . . . four . . . three . . . two . . . Motor please!'

Crouching by the control panel, Spike moved the appropriate switch. The whine of the motor swelled up and filled the cabin. I felt the palms of my hands become clammy with sweat. The warm metallic smell in the interior of the ship grew more pronounced.

Under the glaring lights Uncle Lachlan's face was deeply lined. Suddenly he rapped out: 'Switch to jets!'

Below us the familiar yet always terrifying roar broke out. The ship began to tremble and sway, and for a moment the lights flickered. Then we seemed to be lifted up on an enormous wave.

'Hold on!' shouted Uncle Lachlan.

I shut my eyes and tried to relax, and before long the terrific upward speed brought unconsciousness. . .

And so we began our journey back to Earth. I was the last to come round after the black-out, of course; but no one felt any ill effects, and we soon settled down to our usual routine—Uncle Lachlan and Professor Hermanoff in the laboratory, observing and calculating, Spike at the controls, Madge in the kitchen, and Janet and I at the radar plotting our course.

'One more reading ought to do,' said Janet. 'Ready?'

'Okay,' I said.

'Time—twelve fifty-eight. Interval—nine point nine-five seconds. Right?'

'I've got it down. Just think—we're nearly ten thousand miles away from Hesikos already!'

'Strictly according to schedule: ten thousand miles per hour. Another twenty-nine hours and we should be landing at Inverard.'

I leaned back in my chair and closed the graph-book. 'I hope nothing goes wrong this time,' I said.

'Why should it?'

'I don't know, Janet. I just wish we were back on Earth!'

'That's natural enough. I expect you're a bit tired, like we all are. It wasn't a rest-cure on Hesikos, was it?'

But I wasn't really tired. It was something else that had come over me—an odd tingling feeling, like the sensation you have before an exam. I wasn't quite sure whether it had a mental or a physical cause.

After a time I mentioned it to Janet.

'That's queer,' she said. 'I didn't want to admit it, but I've had the same kind of feeling for the past few minutes. As if—as if I was passing through a current of electricity.'

'That's it! That's exactly it. . .'

And just as I spoke the radar went blank. The flashes were wiped from the screen as if a curtain had been drawn across it, and the pips which accompanied them gave place to an uneasy silence. At the same time the lights in the cabin began to fade and die. In a few seconds it was as dark as pitch.

The hair crawled at the back of my neck. There was only one comfort. The ship, it appeared, continued to fly normally.

I heard the door of the laboratory open, and Uncle Lachlan came blundering towards us: 'What's gone wrong? What's happened to the lights, Spike?'

'I dunno.' Spike sounded astonished and even a little scared. 'The dials on my switchboard have gone crazy, too!'

It was Professor Hermanoff, coming at my uncle's heels, who found the torch. He switched it on, and we gathered in a silent ring around the control panel, desperately wondering what was going to happen.

Madge ran towards us from the kitchen. 'Wot's the matter, Dr. McKinnon? The lights and my stove are all out of action.'

Uncle Lachlan said he thought something had gone wrong with the electrical circuit. That seemed to satisfy her; but to me the odd thing was that the motor and the jets should still be running.

After a moment Spike pulled himself together. 'Maybe a battery terminal has worked loose. Or

one of the fuses may have gone. Let's have a look
behind the panel.'

Professor Hermanoff held the torch, while Spike
and Uncle Lachlan worked on the screws. I noticed
that Madge was shivering; and I began to feel
bitterly cold myself.

Soon the panelling could be lifted away, and we
looked behind. But the leads and terminals were all
right, and there was nothing wrong with the fuses,
either. Uncle Lachlan and Hermanoff exchanged
troubled glances, and the tingling feeling swept
through me once again, making me hot and cold
by turns.

All at once we heard a chiming sound. It seemed
to be outside the ship and gradually coming closer,
and if I had been scared before I was doubly
scared now. We were on the verge of something terrible. I was sure of it.

Then suddenly I remembered. I blurted out:
'We heard a sound like that on our last journey
home—Professor Bergman and I. He said it might
have to do with cosmic rays.'

Uncle Lachlan nodded. 'I wonder, Hermanoff—
could we be caught in a magnetic field?'

'It is possible. It could account for the failure of
power in the ship.'

The sound was all round us, humming and chiming
like the interior of a power-station: the kind of
twanging noise that goes on when millions of volts
are passing between two poles. In a way it was like
the Electronome, too, on the day the power was
trebled.

'Will it—will it damage the ship?' I asked.

Uncle Lachlan looked anxious. 'I don't know, Jeremy. Scientists have written a lot about electromagnetic fields in space. They have warned travellers that they may be dangerous. But we are the first to encounter one.'

In the light of the torch little beads of moisture glistened on Professor Hermanoff's forehead. 'We are stable enough,' he said, trying, I think, to sound encouraging. 'The rotatory jets don't seem to be affected.'

'They shouldn't be,' returned Spike, sharply. 'They work directly from the motor, which is only started by electricity.'

All we could do was wait. And as we waited the sound grew louder and louder until at last it seemed to invade the very metal of the ship. My nerves were snapping. Janet grew pale, and Madge put an arm about her and held her tight. We didn't know what to expect, that was the trouble; and the noise was unusual and frightening, as if a gigantic flock of wailing birds was threatening us. And the darkness made it worse, though it was lucky we had a torch—and luckier still that it was worked by atomic heat and not by a battery.

Panic began to constrict the muscles in my whole body, and I tried to find some relief in talking. 'Uncle Lachlan,' I said, 'are cosmic rays dangerous?'

'In point of fact we know very little about them,' he answered carefully. 'They attack us continually on Earth, it seems, in the form of radiation, and they do us no harm. But here—focused in a magnetic field and without the screening properties of an atmosphere—well, it may be different.'

He had scarcely finished speaking when Janet put her hands up to her face and cried out: 'I'm frightened, Dr. McKinnon! It's so dark in here, and that awful sound hemming us in. If only we could look outside and see what it is!'

There was hysteria in her voice, and I felt it mounting inside me, too. Madge and Uncle Lachlan tried to comfort her, but she became even more shrill and desperate: 'What if we're caught here for ever? You said it was a magnetic field. Our steel ship may never get away——'

Harshly Uncle Lachlan interrupted: 'It may be called a magnetic field, but you ought to know it's not the same as a magnet.'

'Oh, I don't care!' she flung back at him. 'You're trying to keep something from us. We're all going to die!'

And then it was Spike who seemed to lose control. 'She's right!' he exclaimed. 'Tell us the truth, Dr. McKinnon. We're trapped in space! That's what it is—we're trapped in space!'

My uncle caught his shoulder. 'Believe me, Spike,' he said, quieter now and more in command of his own emotions, 'I don't know. I keep telling you I just don't know.'

But Spike refused to listen. 'If we're going to die,' he said, 'tell us now! Tell us the truth——'

And then a voice ran quietly through my head. All the others were aware of it, too. That was obvious by the way they relaxed and seemed to listen. It was the Voice of Hesikos—the telepathy of Solveg, ruler of the Lost Planet. And this was the thought that came to us: *My friends, have courage. Do not be afraid. The danger will pass . . .* Suddenly I remembered his words as we bade him goodbye: 'In moments of doubt or anxiety, each may help the other.'

We stood there, quiet and hopeful now, inside the small ring of light thrown by the torch. I had been thinking for the past few minutes of the immense dark void outside—and of us, small and insignificant and alone, inside the tiny ship; but I knew at last that we weren't alone and that no matter how far away we were the thoughts of the people of Hesikos would always reach us.

Gradually the twanging began to die away. Madge was smiling. ' I *knew* it would be all right,' she said. 'All the same, I'm thankful it's nearly over.'

And almost as she spoke the lights came on, flickering at first, then bright and steady. Spike swung round. 'And my instruments, too!' he exclaimed. 'They're working again!'

In the end the sound disappeared altogether, like a sad, small memory.

Janet was still pale, and I think she felt ashamed of her fears. I went across and took her arm. 'The radar will be on as well. Let's get cracking. We must find out if our course has altered.'

'Very well, Jeremy.'

Madge looked round the cabin, so different now from the dark and ominous place which a few minutes before had been like a coffin. 'I expect my stove's all right now,' she remarked, cheerfully. 'If it is, I'll have lunch ready in a jiff. After all that we do need something to eat.'

CHAPTER XIX

Otto Schenk Returns

WHATEVER IT was we had encountered—and even Professor Hermanoff and Uncle Lachlan have yet to solve the mystery—it had pushed us off course; but when the Earth began to show on the radar we were only a few minutes behind our original schedule. And as we reached a point two thousand miles above the Earth we had almost, if not quite, made up for lost time.

At one minute to six o'clock on the third day we all assembled near the control panel and fastened our safety-belts.

'All secure?' said Uncle Lachlan. 'Good! In less than a minute now we shall be entering the atmosphere of the Earth. You all know what to expect. I release the parachute in the nose of the ship, and Spike shuts off the rotatory jets. As a result the ship swings round, tail downwards. Then the propelling jets come into action as air-brakes. Ready?'

We told him we were.

'I can 'ardly believe it!' whispered Madge. 'Inverard again, and Jock Ferguson waiting for us!'

There was a tremor in the ship as we touched the

tenuous air of the stratosphere, and friction rapidly increased the temperature of the hull.

'Stand by,' Uncle Lachlan said and released the parachute.

The ship heeled over. Loose objects clattered across the deck.

'Spike—cut rotatory jets!'

It was an unpleasant feeling as the whole axis of our existence seemed to shift and we began to slide down the curved hull towards the instrument panel. But everything was normal enough. It was a moment in which you just had to grit your teeth and wait.

'Switch to main jets!'

Presently we heard them, surging up below us and acting as air-brakes. The ship steadied, and the pressure below us became more and more pronounced.

I watched the altimeter. One thousand eight hundred feet . . . one thousand six hundred . . . one thousand three hundred . . .

'Jets off, Spike!'

It was suddenly very quiet. All we could hear was a faint whistle of wind outside.

Six hundred feet . . . three hundred . . . one hundred . . .

'Hold on, everybody!'

I shut my eyes and braced myself. The floor jarred beneath us. For a few seconds the hiss of the hydraulic landing-gear echoed through the cabin, and the ship staggered and swayed. Then there was a startling silence.

Uncle Lachlan blew his nose—'Well,' he remarked,

with a calmness which I don't believe he felt, 'we're home again. Open the main hatch, Jeremy.'

Jock Ferguson and the workmen gave us a great welcome, and reporters swarmed all over the place. For their benefit Uncle Lachlan and Professor Hermanoff recounted the gist of the story.

It was wonderful to lie in bed again and listen to the ripple of the burn in the glen and to the sighing of the pine trees. And in the morning to hear the sparrows chattering outside the window and feel the scent of Charity floating up from the garden. And to eat bacon and eggs at breakfast and just laze and do nothing.

But our adventure wasn't over yet. Next day about twelve o'clock I was passing through the hall when the telephone rang. When I answered it I got the shock of my life. The caller was Otto Schenk. His voice was somehow quieter and kindlier than before, but the smooth guttural accent was unmistakable.

He asked who I was, and when I told him he went on: 'No doubt you are surprised to hear from me. Would you tell Dr. McKinnon that at the moment I am at Renfrew Airport, having flown from Berlin this morning? I have hired a car to take me to Inverard at once and should be with you in the afternoon—about four.'

'Very well, Herr Schenk.'

'Professor Harmenoff is there, too, I believe?'

'Yes.'

'Good. I have something to say to them both. Au revoir, Jeremy.'

I put the receiver down, puzzled and at a loss, wondering why he should suddenly have decided to visit us. We were opposed to all he stood for—strife and greed and bitterness. He was our enemy: our *beaten* enemy, which made him all the more dangerous. And yet it occurred to me that he might have changed. He hadn't sounded angry or bitter on the phone; rather the reverse. And I remembered that once upon a time, until the influence of Hesikos captured him, Professor Hermanoff, too, had been our enemy.

The clock in the library was chiming four when Otto Schenk was ushered in by Janet. She left again at once to tell Madge to bring some tea, leaving him alone with Uncle Lachlan, Professor Hermanoff and myself.

He sat down with a sigh of satisfaction. He had been travelling since early in the morning and was, he said, very tired. I noticed that his slant eyes were no longer wary.

Hermanoff coughed. 'You have something important to say to us?'

'I have.' He smiled a little. 'In the past Dr. McKinnon has turned down several of my—proposals, but this one is different.'

My uncle smiled, too. 'In what way, Herr Schenk?'

'I still think we could work together, you and I. One of the greatest scientists in the world, and one of the richest men. If Professor Hermanoff would join us, it would be even better.'

'Jeremy and I gave you our answer to that proposal not so very long ago.'

'Circumstances have changed, Dr. McKinnon. And my purpose has changed. Something happened to me that day on Hesikos, when the Voice came and I was afraid.'

It was still and quiet outside, and a breath of autumn air flowed in through a half-open window. Somewhere on the moor a grouse was calling.

'What have you in mind?' asked Uncle Lachlan.

Otto Schenk's eyes grew bright and eager. 'I wish to found an Institute for Peace—an Institute to point the way to peace through scientific achievement.'

'But that would require unlimited money and time,' put in Professor Hermanoff, quickly.

'I have money—sufficient to launch my scheme at any rate. And when I give up my armament firms I shall have plenty of time as well. What do you say? You shall be the first Director of the Institute, Dr. McKinnon. And you, Professor Hermanoff, Deputy. A Briton and a Russian—and I, a German, as Secretary. Think of it! New discoveries, new inventions, new theories—all harnessed in the cause of peace. An inspiration to all the world.'

There was a long silence, broken at last by Uncle Lachlan. 'Herr Schenk, it is a wonderful project. But we ought to seek further advice—from the United States and India and South America——'

'But of course. My money will only serve as a beginning. I feel sure, however, that other nations will recognise the value of such an Institute and support us.'

My uncle turned to me. 'Jeremy, you have been

very quiet. How does all this appeal to you? It is you—and your generation—who will reap the benefits.'

'This time I'd say yes, Uncle Lachlan.'

He smiled. To Professor Hermanoff he said: 'Would you co-operate?'

'I would pledge my life to such a cause.'

'Then we're with you, Herr Schenk. We can discuss details—later.'

The man who had been our enemy stood up. He caught my uncle's hands and looked at us. 'My friends,' he said, 'today, for the first time, I have found real happiness.'

While they drank their tea and discussed the future I wandered out into the garden. It was a beautiful evening, and I noticed that the flowers of Charity were turning towards the sun.